Torturing Souls

AP Greene

DEDICATION

To all the good girls looking at the bad boys

ACKNOWLEDGMENTS

Jess: Thanks for being the best no questions asked supporter

Kiersten: Thank you for encouraging this dream

Readers: Thank you for letting me share this with all of you

Chapter 1

Daniella
An accountant walks into a mafia-owned bar. It sounds like the beginning of a bad joke, but I'm here because I have questions and I have a feeling Mr. Salvatore Segreto is going to like what I have to offer in exchange for answers to my questions. If I'm being honest, he's making out better than I will be.

I just need to get inside, wait until I can handle the number of guys, aka made men, get them situated, and force one of them to call their boss. Even in my head this sounds a little extreme, but I've tried everything else. With no bouncer, I go right up to the bar and sit where I can keep an eye on the entire bar. Even the pool tables.

"What can I get you?" Looking up at the bartender, I never know what to order. I'm not a drinker, but I can't not drink at a bar if I want to blend in.

"Whiskey and a water, please." Flashing an innocent smile, I hope that's the end of this conversation.

"I haven't seen you in here before. New to the area?"

"I have a client in town." Not a complete lie, Mr. Segreto will be my client by the end of the day.

This seems to pique his interest. "What do you do?" Swirling the whiskey around but not drinking it. "I'm an accountant." "I thought accountants meet with clients during the first quarter for taxes?"

1

He doesn't realize how irked that makes me. "I don't do taxes. Much to everyone's shock, accountants do more than just taxes and audits. I specialize in consulting work. Fraud investigations mainly. I've been in more courtrooms than some lawyers." It's times like this when I really wish I could stomach alcohol. He's getting under my skin so easily and I need a clear head to handle all of this. Luckily, he picks up on my agitation and moves to the other side of the bar. If two more guys leave, I'll be able to get the boss here without having to discretely get rid of this whiskey since the bartender is keeping one eye on me now.

After finishing my water, I realize it's time. When the bartender goes to the bathroom, I quickly tie up all the men while disarming them. If they don't tell me what Mr. Segreto's number is, they are knocked out. So far, all of them have kept their mouth shut. The bartender though is already calling someone when he sees me holding a gun to one of the men's head. After hanging up, "Mind if I drink this?" Shaking my head, I watch him down my whiskey

***

"Why was I called in the middle of the night? It better" his voice stops when he takes in the scene. Me playing pool, the bartender handcuffed to the bar and the rest of the men knocked unconscious.

"Glad you could make it, Mr. Segreto. It would be best if you could leave your remaining men outside so we can talk." Looking at the bartender, I unlock the cuffs and tell him to leave, which he does while muttering an apology to his boss.

Once it is just the two of us, "Who are you and why shouldn't I kill you for harming my men?"

Sighing, I knew this was what he was going to say. So predictable. "You can kill me but then you wouldn't figure out who is stealing from your organization. I, on the other hand, can help you find that person. All I would like in exchange is some honest answers." Going behind the bar, I grab myself another water and pour him something from a bottle before pushing it across the bar. "Don't worry, all the men in here can't hear a thing."

After taking a healthy sip, "Why do you think there is a person stealing from my organization?"

"Because some of your companies have been slowly losing money even though revenues are up and expenses have remained steady." I give him the bottle I poured out of and go sit on the other side of the bar. I just can't tell him how I found out this information. "I have no interest in your money or what you do that might be frowned upon by others. I just need some answers." Hopefully, I don't play all my cards so he can trick me.

Looking at me like he can see my soul, I hold his stare. "I'll look into your claim and contact you if I think we can be helpful to each other." That's better than being shot outright, both figuratively and literally. I nod, pull out my business card and leave it on the bar with my tab.

"Cell's on the back, not that you couldn't have someone get it for you. To protect yourself, I'd keep this information between us so you don't spook the thief." With that, I make my way out of the bar and start driving to the hotel I'm staying in. I don't mind the guys trailing me. Mr. Segreto is going to have all my information within an hour, so I don't care.

**

I wake with a start and notifications. *"Let's discuss at my office at dinner. 6pm."* With an address link. I look at the clock and see it's already 8am. I've always been a morning person and I need to get some work done if I'm going to be killed tonight at dinner.

I neglected a lot of work after Alex died until I found that note. Now that I have a plan, I always work better. After getting dressed and grabbing breakfast from downstairs, I get started.

Checking the clock, I see it's already time to prep for this meeting and eat before getting dressed. Driving to the office, I'm not surprised it's a high rise in downtown. Not that I didn't research it before leaving. As I'm pulling into the underground parking lot, I notice there are only a few cars. Nothing like being a small female in a dark parking garage with few witnesses.

Once I'm in the lobby I go to the security guard who is too well-dressed. "Hello." I wait for him to look up. "I have a meeting with Mr. Segreto at 6pm."

After grunting, he walks me to the elevators and assesses me from head to toe. "Are you the one who knocked my friends out?"

I consider telling the truth, but in this case being underestimated is in my best interest. Feigning confusion, "What are you talking about?" Now, more grunts. I guess I need to learn grunt language. With my knowledge of corporations and research of mafias, this is going to be a huge boy's club. They probably only have women working as secretaries. Possibly not even then since they don't want their women thinking they are cheating.

"Boss is in the office with the light on. Everyone else has gone home for the day."

With that, I make my way to the farthest possible office. At least it is an open floor plan with offices around the border. I knock at the door even though he was probably told I was here and watched me on the security cameras.

"I'm glad you came. I didn't want to hunt you down." I don't know what to say to that. Thank you for not shooting me? Well, wait until you hear my questions? "Please, have a seat. I had a simple dinner prepared. Also, nobody is going to interrupt us, but." He places a small device on the table and turns it on.

"Recorder or scrambler?" I ask as I sit down. At least neither of us have our backs to the door. He might trust his men, but I don't.

Smirking, he lifts the lid of my plate before removing his. "Scrambler. Why would I want this recorded? I also don't want to search you to see if you are wearing a wire so this will be just as effective."

I look at the grilled cheese and tomato soup in front of me and am instantly happy I ate before. Nothing like explaining how an Italian is lactose intolerant. "I need you to trust me so if you want to search me that's fine." I shrug so he knows it truly isn't an issue. Why lie? "Why am I here?" I sit back and pick up the wine glass before looking for the wet bar, which I find in the corner.

"We need to discuss how you are going to do your investigation without my men asking too many questions. I also want answers, but I know you need access to all the books, which I am fine with. I need to know what questions you will ask so I can find answers before you finish your task." He watches me go over to the wet bar and grab a glass and fill it with water. "Do you not drink?"

"No, I don't. The plan is simple. I assume you are over 40 since you have two adult sons. So, I'll be evaluating your companies to help you with estate planning. Everyone will answer my questions when they realize I'm not an enemy nor am I trying to steal their jobs. If you say I'm an auditor, problems. I don't like problems. I need open information and people to trust me inherently; not with issued threats."

After I finish my drink, I refill it before returning to the table. "Have you done this before?" He asks, even though I'm sure he knows.

"Helped a mafia boss or hid in plain sight to find fraud? No and yes. I have been in this industry long enough to know what to do and say so I can be most effective."

"What's wrong with the food I had prepared for you." It's not a question. No, we have moved onto demands. I remember to not roll my eyes. But I look at his almost empty plate.

"I ate before I came." Not a lie, but he just stares.

"But you were invited for dinner." Great, he's mad.

Guess he didn't like my simple answer. "I can't eat dairy." That explains the sandwich. Now how to explain the soup? Instead of answering the unasked question, I walk to his window, which is the entire back of his office.

"You don't trust me even though you came to me. I don't harm women." Like that is going to get me to open up. "I couldn't find anything about your past before age 16. Why." Again, another demand, not a question.

"I trust you to not harm me. Your men, a different story. Why do you want to know about my past? I'm just a consultant. I'll be out of here as soon as we are both satisfied." I continue giving him my back.

"What questions do you need answers to?" When I don't answer right away, he comes and stands at his desk, which is directly behind me.

I look up at the stars like I always do when I think of Alex. "I need to know why my brother was targeted for a mob hit. He's the one who somehow found out there was fraud in your organization. I just confirmed it before bringing it to you. Your family was the only one who didn't send a

5

representative to his funeral."

"What's your brother's name and when did he die?"

"Alex and two weeks ago tomorrow." I say without any emotion because if I start, I will cry through Mr. Segreto's shirt. I see him pull out his phone.

"Why do you think it was a mob hit?" The one question I knew was coming but hoped didn't.

Before I answer, I decide if the truth is worth it. "Because I was there." He doesn't need to know what happened to me or what I saw.

"Can you start tomorrow? I have an open office across from mine that you can use. You can let me know what you need. I will have a computer set up for you and IT will be here for questions." Down to business. I like this guy. Plus, he doesn't ask more questions about that night.

"Sure. What time?"

"We typically start at 9, but if you want to come in at a different time, we can make something work." For the first time, he seems cautious and uncertain. I'm sure nobody else sees this side of him.

"I'll be in at 8. I'm a morning person, so the earlier the better. I will need to meet with the head of the organizations." When I look at him, he's confused. "I'm sure someone runs each company individually instead of having you run each one." When he nods, I continue. "I need to know who runs each company and how they are handled. Do you have cross over between companies or are they all run separately? I assume there would be cross over with personnel which would result with the subsidiaries..." I trail off when I see his eyes glaze over. Great. "Does one of your sons run some of the companies?"

"Yes. Are you telling me they shouldn't be together?" I can't tell if he's offended or confused.

"I assumed there would be cross over. It makes the most sense with the size of the overall organization. Can you set up a meeting with your son for me tomorrow morning? It will make it easier if I can find out a starting point. I'll see you tomorrow morning."

I turn to leave and get halfway before I hear a safety click. "You think my sons are behind this." I stand still as I feel the gun against my head. So much for not harming a woman.

I turn so I'm facing the gun. If he's going to shoot me, he's going to look me in the eyes. "No. It doesn't make sense for them to steal as they would eventually take over. That is why I want to meet with one of them or both. I don't care who it is. If they can answer questions to my satisfaction, I don't have to keep asking you. I mean this is as nicely as possible, but I think you are too far removed to be overly helpful in an investigation into the underlying records." I hold myself steady while he thinks this over. When he finally lowers his gun, I pull mine out. "Next time, you might want to search me because I shoot first."

With that, I walk out of his office and go straight to my car. I don't care that another black SUV is now across from my car. My drive to the hotel is uneventful except for the SUV tailing me. I'm tempted to have him try to stay with me, but I just want my pajamas and sleep. I have to be back bright and early tomorrow. Usually, I have a few days to prepare. Mr. Segreto seems very impatient.

Chapter 2

Tony

"Meet me at the office, now." Reading the text and seeing the time does not bode well. I'm used to my job operating mostly at night, but getting a text from my father, who runs the family business, at this time is never good. Heads are going to roll.

Luckily, I don't have a bed mate to kick out tonight. Trying to kick them out in the past has never been an easy task. Quickly dressing, there is no time to shower when you are told now by the head of this family. Even though he does everything for family, I wouldn't put it past him to shoot his own son.

After texting back that I was on my way. I get to the office in no time at this hour. The security guard, or soldier, buzzes me in, without a second hesitation. I go straight to my dad's office and Matteo is already there. Both have glasses of something that they are drinking. It doesn't look like this is either of theirs's first.

As soon as I close the door. "We have a problem." Dad was never one for words. It's not uncommon for us to have problems with the type of business we are in, but dad seems off and Matteo isn't his typical smug self, which tells me this is bigger than my normal fix-it problems.

"What do I need to do? Do you have a name already?" I can have a person's full life story within a day. My second will find them and bring them to a location where I get to know them personally. I might have an MBA, which I use to help run multiple companies in our family's business, but my true joy comes from my not-so-legitimate duties.

"I have two names. One is going to help us figure out who the problem is. I've discussed this with Matteo. You will assist her in the investigation. The other is a dead man who was apparently killed by someone who runs in our circle." While he is talking, he hands me a folder with a business card in it. This is more than just a photo at least.

"Why couldn't this wait until normal hours?" I ask even though I know better. But come on, it's the middle of the night and now I'm going to be dead on my feet when I have fun planned for this evening. My second is closing in on an issue which means I have to deal with that tonight. I'm going to need a nap in the afternoon so I can have the patience I need.

"Because someone is stealing from us." My head snaps up quickly enough that I'm surprised it's still attached to my body. Nobody is stupid enough to steal from our family. Even though it has never been confirmed, it's not a secret that we have illegitimate businesses and are part of the criminal underground. "Exactly, so this stays between the three of us. Plus, the new girl. But nobody else hears a word of this."

Looking at Matteo, he's back to his normal self. "What is the cover for this girl?" He always knows what questions to ask which is why he will be a great boss one day when dad retires. Thankfully, I'll just step in as the underboss, which he currently is.

When it's clear dad isn't going to answer. Matteo stands. "Alright, if that's everything, I left someone keeping my bed warm who I'd like to return to before I have to be here in less than four hours to meet this person." I don't think he goes a single day without someone in his bed, but it's always a different person. I don't know how he hasn't run out of options. New York City is big, but I don't know if it's that big. For a time, he was seeing the same guy. I got to meet him once, but he went off the rails a few weeks ago and hasn't mentioned him since.

Once he's gone, I look at my father before nodding and standing to leave. "I'm going to need her information first. I have a meeting with her here at 6pm to go over everything and a game plan for how to make sure she can get the information out of everyone without scaring the thief." That makes sense. I look at the business card, if she's only involved in legitimate business, it shouldn't be that difficult.

"As long as this is her real name, I should be able to meet with you at lunch with all my findings." As soon as I make it to the door, I realize something. "How did you find out about this?"

Now this gets me a full smile. "She tied up every soldier off duty at our bar, then handcuffed Rob to the bar after he called me when he saw all the men tied up. I showed up and we had a nice little chat where many threats were given."

Also, how big is woman if she overpowered made men? That takes balls. I don't think half of the people in our family would ever try something like that. But that just shows how desperate she is and for some reason, I really need to meet this woman. "Why are you smiling?'

As soon as the words leave my mouth, his smile disappears. "It's been a while since anybody surprised me like she did. Ten made men, tied up with shoe laces all knocked out. The crazy part was she gave me her back multiple times. Almost like she knew she was safe even though many have died for less."

***

Even though Matteo went home and I should as well, I'm up and here so I might as well get that information for dad so I can have a nice nap before my other job starts.

I pour a big cup of coffee and get started on my background check. Nothing to crazy, I find her business site, college transcripts, driver's license, no run-ins with the law except a few minor traffic tickets. Everything about her is normal.

I keep searching hoping to find something exciting because normal puts me to sleep and I was running on fumes when I started. I stare at my screen. This can't be right. Why would she change her name as soon as she turned 16? I start searching her birth name and finally, something interesting. I find her brother's and parents' obituaries. However, I know him.

Once I look into the three of them, something isn't adding up. They were all killed. Not car accidents, not some illness. Murdered. But no police reports showing they were investigated. Their obituaries don't say how they were killed, just 'taken too soon'. No autopsy reports which mean someone knows how they were killed and why and didn't want that information in the wrong hands.

I start investigating her brother since I already found out everything about her. What's interesting is a familiar number keeps popping up in his phone records right before his death. I'm going to need to warn Matteo. Maybe even talk to Daniella first to find out how they knew each other. I should give him a head's up in case he knows her.

***

I drop off my folder of findings on the girl only to my dad, which was quick since he had someone in a meeting. One plus of being in this organization, no questions are asked when a folder is handed off with no explanation even though you interrupt what could be an important meeting. Nobody is stupid enough to question the boss.

Entering my brother's office after knocking but not waiting for a response is usually the easiest way to get shot. I know because he's shot me before. Luckily, doc was on site and it was an easy through and through. Dad was pissed. Smirking at the memory, I close the door and pour us both a drink. We are going to need it when I start asking questions.

"What. Some of us have things to do during the day." He grunts. Honestly, he's been like this for a few weeks, but now that I know why, I brush off his attitude.

"We need to talk about what happened in dad's office this morning." With that, he actually stops typing and looks at me before grabbing a scrambler from his drawer. You would think nobody would be stupid enough to bug any of these offices, but we like to air on the side of caution. Well, paranoia is probably more accurate.

We know each other well enough that I know he doesn't need to prompt me before I hand him a folder, just like the one I gave dad. "He was your partner, which explains why you've been so grumpy the last two weeks. Who killed him?"

11

Matteo and I are less than 2 years apart. When mom left, we became even closer. Being in this family meant needing to know who you can trust. We both know we can call each other with no judgment or worry. When he brought a guy to a simple dinner at my place, I didn't ask any questions and just pulled out another plate. In our business, most don't take well to anything non-traditional. After our mother, we both just wanted the opposite of what our dad had with her. So, between the two of us, we don't care who the other is with as long as they are happy. Plus, it's not frowned upon to shoot a man if they break someone's heart, but it is a problem to shoot a woman.

"How did you find him? I thought he was just ghosting me." The first part is shock and the second is more to himself than anything else.

"This is the girl's brother. While doing my search, I found his obituary and decided that I should look into him further. Especially his death. Did you tell him the truth?" I honestly don't know how serious they were. Bringing him to my place could be a check to see if I find anything wrong that he can't see. We've done that before to each other. Well, that was the only time since neither of us are relationship people. Or it could have been him wanting us to meet since they are at the stage of meeting the families.

Sighing, he looks at the ceiling like all the answers are there. "I didn't tell him outright, but he was putting pieces together. Especially after I showed up covered in blood with a gunshot wound. He didn't ask, but he patched me up while waiting for doc. He wasn't stupid and I didn't hide anything. Maybe I should've. Because if his death was because of me, I don't know how I'll explain that to his sister."

For the first time I am doubting myself. Maybe I shouldn't have told him because he will definitely assume it is all his fault and never date again. Hell, he might even ask dad to arrange a marriage. Yes, in our world it isn't that uncommon. "Did you ever meet his sister?"

"Yeah. We were…" For the first time since we became made men, Matteo looks terrified. "Dad's going to find out and kill me. How am I supposed to hide how I know her when she comes here?" He gets up and starts pacing.

Taking a deep breath, one of us has to be level headed and now I have to tell him the one thing he never wanted to know. "Dad knows." I say just above a whisper like this secret is too much for the world.

"What do you mean? Did you tell him?" He points his pistol at me.

The door flies open and dad is standing there. "Why are you pointing a gun at Tony?" He's pissed. Dad doesn't like when we fight or pull weapons on one another. Standing up for the other, different story.

Knowing Matty won't lower the gun until I answer. I talk even though dad is glaring at me. "No, I didn't." I don't say more than I want to. Honestly, how did he think dad wasn't going to figure out he had men stay the night at his place? I'm sure dad has either soldiers watching our places or has live feed into our security systems. This is why I recommend staying at their place and never bring someone to mine. He can ask why I didn't go home but there are more than enough reasons I can use as an answer.

Matteo lowers his gun and puts it back in the holster. "Are you going to tell me what that was about?" When we both shake our heads, he continues. "During your search, did you find anything that she might want answers to? Our deal will be, she finds the thief and I get her answers. So, I'd like to know what questions she might want to know before I agree to anything tonight."

Knowing Matteo is going to be pissed about this I keep my eyes on him. "Her brother was killed not too long ago. It looks like it was a hit. No autopsy even though one was requested. No police report or investigation." I hate lying to my dad, but I can't say why it might have been a hit. That's going to have to come from Matteo.

With a slight nod, I get ready to separate dad and Matteo because he is getting ready to tell dad his secret. "It's my fault." He says it so softly that I doubt anyone could hear that confession.

"What is your fault? And why?" One thing about dad is he never jumps to conclusions. He loves to gather information and make an informed decision. It's probably why he is the longest don out of the five families.

"Because I was dating him. So, he obviously was killed to get to me. They probably wanted information and figured he'd be the weakest link." Great, he's back to pacing. I don't know if it's because dad officially knows or because it's his greatest fear, falling for someone only for them to be taken

13

because of who we are.

"Did you meet his sister?" When he nods, dad just looks at me. "Find out why he was killed and who did it. Also, you will be dealing with her. Not Matteo." When he reaches the door, I figure we're in the clear, but he stops with his hand on the knob. "Next time, bring him over so I can meet my son's partner." He doesn't wait for a response, but he shuts the door on his way out.

Looking at Matteo, I leave so he can gather himself.

***

I needed this assignment after dealing with Matteo today. Mario is sitting in a chair watching the target who is now strung up with his feet barely touching the ground.

After finishing up my assignment, I get a call. "Hey dad, what's up?" After he fills me in on his meeting with the consultant, I get her cover story for our purposes.

"She's an estate planner. She'll be making sure everything is in order for my estate." My dad chuckles, which he hasn't done since mom left. Twenty years and I haven't seen him smile fully or laugh, but now, faced with someone stealing from us, he laughs.

"Are you dying? Why do you need an estate planner?" I ask because honestly that's going to be everyone's question. There is no retiring in this business, you leave once you make it to the grave.

"In our line of work, you should always be prepared to not make it home." Suddenly serious and I get it, he's had a will his entire life and once Matty and I turned 18, we had wills drawn up too. With that, he hangs up and I go home to shower.

Chapter 3

Daniella

I know he said I could start at 9, but waiting until 8 was going to be hard enough. It's 7:30 and I'm sitting in the parking garage waiting until it is an acceptable time to go in. I start looking at the notes Alex left to try to piece more information together with what I know now.

I keep looking at the envelope with Matteo's name on it. As soon as I entered Mr. Segreto's office and saw the picture of the two boys, I knew Alex's partner was his son. I might actually be able to give him the letter that Alex left. I've been carrying it around since his death, along with a small box. That I won't give anyone until I know Matteo felt the same about Alex that he did.

I remember the day Alex told me about the ring he bought for his partner. I squealed and insisted we have a dinner together so I could make sure he was good enough. He won me over so quickly. It wasn't anything he said since he was quiet and seemed so uncomfortable. He tracked my brother when he stood up, offered to help him – not me – and his eyes. The biggest tell are always their eyes. When he looked at me, they were cold, almost like he had seen too much and couldn't be bothered with people. But when he turned those eyes onto Alex, they melted, it was the first time that I knew Alex would be safe and taken care of.

I reach for my coffee and find a large man staring into my car. Hands cupped onto the glass and everything. I don't say anything as I take a sip and lower the window.

"Hi, are you planning to stay down here all day? My job is to escort you up to the floor and show you around." With that, he turns and walks towards the elevators. This is going to be weird. He's dressed in a full suit. The kind you wear to a wedding or funeral.

I gather my stuff and follow him into the elevators. Just because I'm a morning person does not mean I'm talkative in the morning. I focus better in the morning when the rest of the world is quiet. Probably because there are no expectations of what is to occur.

He shows me to an office and hands me a badge. Luckily, no names or titles. He starts up the computer and hands me a paper with credentials. "Mr. Segreto said you have a meeting with Tony. He is already here, so whenever you get settled, you can go across the hall, four doors down. He has his lights on, so you shouldn't miss it." Then, he turns and leaves. He was probably told I was here when I tried to enter the parking garage. I didn't see any other cars though.

Grabbing a new notepad, pen, and my coffee, I make my way to Tony's office. Hopefully he isn't the one stealing because if it is him, this will be a short assignment.

I knock on the open door. I'm met with steely eyes void of emotion assessing my body from top to bottom and back up. I hold his gaze. After the number of years in this profession, one thing you get used to is being assessed.

At least he is attractive. That might not be the best word though. Styled hair, before he ran his hands through it too much, piercing grey eyes, muscular arms in a fitted dress shirt. Damn. I can get used to this. When I finish my assessment, he smirks. "Like what you see?" As if he doesn't know how captivating he is?

I'm not a fan of male egos, so I smirk myself. "I've seen better, but I can admire bed head." Based on the rest of his appearance, he doesn't like to not be put together. I take the seat across from him after shutting the door.

He pulls out a device just like his dad did last night. They are paranoid. It makes sense. They are a huge crime family, but I wonder what his role is though. He's younger than Matteo, so I assume his brother would take over. I guess he's the under-underboss?

He hands me a piece of paper with company names and a person's name. There must be over 25 companies. "I handle most of the companies. Matteo is transitioning some more to me, but Hal and Fred are in charge of the rest. Obviously, it's not me or my brother."

"How long have Hal and Fred been with the corporation? Also, are there a lot of cross over between staff and procedures from one company to the next?"

"Hal grew up with my dad and they came up through the ranks together. Fred joined about 10 years ago? He joined after his son was murdered by another family. As for procedures, everything is under the family business, so everyone works together and things are handled as they are expected to be handled."

I'm not enjoying this cryptic shit. I don't know what expectations they have. I'm not a mind reader. "Ok, that didn't answer my question at all. Do you have a company handbook? How things should be recorded? Who has access to bank statements, corporate credit cards, control overrides?" I get a glassy eyed look back at me. This is going to be harder than I thought. "Let's start with an easy one. Did you get a college degree?" He nods looking confused with the sudden change. "What is it in?"

"Standard MBA. My dad wanted me to have an understanding of how things should go once Matteo is promoted." He grins like it's a great accomplishment. I have a feeling he slept through his classes and fucked the professor to get a good grade.

"Did you have to take accounting?" He nods again; no longer proud of his degree. "Did you fuck your professor?" I don't know why he wouldn't have some understanding. He's basically the CEO of multiple companies. He should have some understanding of the words I'm saying.

"First time I've been accused of sleeping with my teacher in the first meeting with someone." He seems amused now. "I understood everything you said and asked. We don't have a handbook, but we do have written procedures. Only five people have admin control on our system and that is the four CEOs, for a lack of better term, and my father."

"Alright, I'll need a copy of the written procedures as well as admin access. I should be able to see overrides easily without disrupting or someone seeing. Are you typically in the office or should I ask Matteo any questions? Or your father?"

"I'll send over that information when I get it. I'm your liaison, so I'll be here when you need me to be."

Without another word, I leave him so I can get started. Nothing like a good hunt to get your blood pumping.

***

Getting lost in accounting records is what every investigator wants. I have been through the financial statements for all the companies and I think I see a pattern. I went back five years and it looks just like Alex wrote. Somehow the expenses are increasing, small amounts, but noticeable in a majority of the companies.

I look up and realize the day is almost done. I created lists of things to investigate further as I was going through the statements. But now that it's just scribbles, I type it out and print it. This I can take home and come up with a game plan.

I send Tony an email saying I won't need to meet with him first thing tomorrow. I figure at least staying on his good side for now and not making him come in early each day when I don't need him would be beneficial for when we do find this guy.

He wasn't happy when I turned down his offer for lunch and dinner. I held up my lunch pail and he just returned later and asked about dinner. I lied and said I had something cooking at the hotel. Who cooks in their hotel room? There is no point in starting something when I most likely won't be around in a year or so. After Alex was killed, I found out there is a hit on my head. The only good thing is nobody knows who I truly am. The last family member I had that knew my truth was just killed.

I can't let Tony close to me because he might end up just like my brother. Matteo on the other hand, he might want to know me since he was with my brother. It would be easier if I could keep him close so I can keep him safe.

18

***

One thing that is the same in New Jersey and New York City, diners are everywhere. Alex told me all about his favorite diner that he and Matteo went to all the time. Apparently, it was in a safe area where his partner wouldn't be found. I just didn't know his partner was the son to one of the heads of a mafia family. My parents were traditional, but after everything, we didn't care about traditions. Just be happy. That was our motto. He found his person right before he was killed.

I should be shocked Matteo is here, but knowing Alex, I'm not. It was a long first day and I needed something that reminded me of him, so I came to the one place he couldn't get enough of. No, I didn't order his favorite meal because that would be weird. But, Matteo did. I don't think he even knows I'm here. I look at my phone so I just look like a bored girl as he makes his way to the exit.

I should mind my business and not check on him. "We should have taken care of him as well as the other one." It's spoken softly. I did get the nickname rabbit ears from Alex. I can hear too much, which bothers me. Typically, I block it all out. But in the city with my back to the door, I made sure to keep them open. I don't like the shuffling sound of people throwing money before stalking out, but when I look over, it is definitely the guys I heard talking about killing someone.

I quickly leave cash to cover my meal and follow after them. I get in my car and trail them. They seem to be getting a little too close to Matteo. I don't owe him anything, but Alex would come back, kill me, and then lecture me. As much as I miss him, he shouldn't worry about my values. At least Matteo is able to tell he's being followed and loses the two guys.

Once we are in a somewhat remote area, I get in front of them and feign car trouble. They stop and even turn off their car before getting out. I wave, "Hey, do either of you know cars?"

"I'm sure we can help you out." I can hear the smugness of his voice. After the one is close enough, the other pulls out his phone. "Hey, something came up. I'll let you know when we can meet." Goodie, now whoever they had plans with won't be looking for them and I can take my time.

After using the stun gun on the close one, the other rounds the raised

19

hood, before getting stunned like his buddy. I somehow get them into cuffs and into the back seat.

The first thing I did after getting a list of all the companies and who ran them, was run the assets, specifically buildings. Just in case. I knew they would have warehouses for questioning. I start driving there while calling the one number I saved for this assignment. Sent to voicemail three times so I leave a message. "Hi. I answered one of my questions you are supposed to answer. I'm taking them to one of your assets, so I can get more."

I pull into the empty lot and take a deep breath. How am I supposed to get them strung up inside? I stun them again so they don't wake up and get away and go look for a cart or rolling chair.

After getting them all strung up, they start singing. It's lovely. I get all the answers I know they have. I didn't even get a drop of blood on my outfit. I sit back and wait. I can't kill them. Not literally, I can kill. I just don't want to start problems with the family I'm assisting and I'm sure they are going to have some questions for my new friends. Hopefully I can keep them alive long enough for someone to come and make decisions.

After a few hours of waiting, I start playing music. I need something to keep me awake. If I fall asleep, they could die. I should have brought snacks, but I honestly didn't expect to either capture them or not have my calls go to voicemail. I'm also not a night person; I'm better in the morning. As soon as a good dance song comes on, I get up and start dancing. These two won't live long enough to tell people how awful I am at dancing. I hear the door slide open, I grab one of the guns and dive behind the table.

"Oh. Someone brought us a present." "I feel bad. We didn't bring them one." I don't recognize the voices, so I slowly poke my head above the table. They don't even know I'm here. "Someone started without us."

"Excuse me." I wait for them to turn. Of course, guns are drawn. "I'm not here to cause problems, but could either of you get ahold of the boss man or even one of his sons? Actually, can you make sure Matteo is alright?"

Neither of them says a word, but their guns do start to lower. "I'm not going to shoot you. I just need some guidance, but I think others will have more questions. They have been quite helpful so far." I smile a true smile. Not one of my fake ones.

They whisper and I turn off my music. One pulls his phone out and starts talking quickly. "Alright. You want to tell me how you knew this place existed?" The other one asks.

"Would if I could. That's not my choice." I remain quiet. I'm not giving more information than required and right now, they can't do anything.

"All three will be here in a few minutes. Honestly, this is going to be the best show I've seen in a while." Both of them pull chairs over to the table and join me while we wait.

Chapter 4

Tony

I had no words when my work was interrupted. I don't like to be interrupted, but when they said my father was requesting me at another location and to wait until he arrives, my interest piqued.

I didn't have to wait long, but I wasn't expecting Matteo to be here. He's never been a fan of the work that occurs in the warehouses. For all three of us to be here is a rarity and not something I like. Something big is about to happen.

"What's going on dad?" I ask since it looks like Matteo is about to fall asleep meanwhile, I'm wide awake.

My dad looks pissed. "Apparently, a woman brought us presents." The only reason I don't pull my gun out is my father hasn't and nobody is as fast as him at drawing. Plus, this is our building. Only our guys are inside. Except this mystery woman. No woman, that I know of, has ever stepped foot inside.

I freeze once I take in the scene. Two soldiers are laughing at the table. Two other made men, not our family, are hanging from the ceiling. Neither are shocking, no, it's the consultant that is sitting on the table with our soldiers.

My dad walks right up to the table and glares at her. "Hi, thank you so much for coming. I didn't really know what to do when you didn't answer my calls." As if that is acceptable. Nobody talks to him like that. "So, these are the two guys that killed my brother. Not that you care, I'm sure. However, what should concern you is they told me they were also supposed to kill Matteo. Now, I don't know much about your family, but my brother would kill me if I didn't step in. So, when I saw these two goons following your son home from a diner, I figured I should see what was going on."

She just stops talking like that is more than enough reason. I'm thrilled she stopped them from killing my brother, but why were they targeting him? Also, why were all four of them at the same diner? I do notice that she didn't out my brother to my father or the soldiers. My dad just continues to stare at her like he's trying to figure something out, but he's missing too many pieces.

I'm more worried about Matteo because he is slowly getting closer and closer to the two men and he has murder in his eyes. I look at my dad hoping he can be of some help, but everyone seems in a trance. "You two can go." I say to the soldiers. No need for them to hear everything. "Dad, you might want to stop Matteo." Nope, no glance at us; he's locked in. "Dad!"

"What." He snaps, but it gets him to look over. "Matteo, not yet. You will get your revenge, but we need answers. I want to know why they are targeting you." He says it nicer than I've heard from him in a while.

"Don't worry. I got those answers already." She waves a piece of paper. "Here are my notes of everything that they said. I wanted to make sure it was all true." She hands my brother the paper.

"Why didn't you kill them?" That makes everyone look at me. I mean, it's a reasonable question.

"Since I didn't know if the two of them are part of your world, I didn't want to make decisions that could impact you. Also, it's not my kill." The first part was to my dad, but the second was to my brother.

"He was your brother." Matteo says. I know he wants to end them, but I know he's thinking she deserves it more than him. He still feels guilty for not knowing he was killed.

"I had my fun. Trust me, Alex would want you to be able to say goodbye." Matteo looks to my dad. He knows the impact of killing made men, but they killed his person and targeted him. My dad just nods.

Now that it is an acceptable kill, Matteo looks at the tools laid out to deal with them. "I'll take you home." I say to Daniella. She doesn't need to see this.

"I drove," she says as she starts leaving, but she stops at Matteo. "Whatever you do, he won't judge you." I don't think she realizes how much he needed to hear that.

I follow her outside and note her shock. I chuckle when she faces me full of fury. I've seen scarier kittens. But as she gets ready to yell at me, I notice she looks just like she did when she walked in the office this morning. "How are you not covered in blood and dirt? You pulled two men, twice your size, into your car and then into the warehouse. Then you tortured them."

I don't know if that was the right thing to say because she smirks. She's naturally stunning, like the girl next door, but when she smirks, it turns everything on. "I'm efficient in everything I do. Where is my car? I'm guessing one of your 'friends' took it."

Ah, that brain. When she started telling me about basic accounting and finance, which I know better than most, it took everything in me not to haul her across my desk. "Yes. They are checking it out to make sure you couldn't be tracked or anything. I'll drive you home." I say as I open the passenger door.

"Are you still staying at the Four Seasons?" I ask, but when I look at her, she's asleep. How can you torture two guys and fall asleep? I'm about to turn away from the docks when a call comes in and she jumps up. "What." It's been too long of a day and I know nothing good is coming out of this call.

"Uh boss, they're ready to talk, but only to you." No names, nothing that can be wired and used.

"I'll be there in twenty. I have to drop something off first." I don't take my eyes off the road even though I feel her stare.

"I don't think they have that long honestly."

"It's fine. We can go there first." After that, I hang up. "I'd like to know how you got so messy. I'm good at getting people to open up, which is why I had all my answers within ten minutes." That's all she says before leaning back in her seat.

"Maybe I'll let you have a turn when they change their minds." We drive back to the warehouses in peace. Her about to fall asleep, but I now want to get answers as quick as possible. She deserves to rest. I pull into the lot and park. When I open her door after checking the area, I have to wake her up again. I should just leave her here and handle everything. As I'm about to text one of the soldiers inside to wait with her, she yawns and steps out.

"I'm fine, let's get this over with. I have a date tonight."

I stop in my tracks. A date? With whom and when? That's not happening. "With who?" I know she's going to correct me.

She looks back at where I'm frozen by the car door. "McPillow and DJ blanket. They are great. You should definitely check them out."

I laugh, completely forgetting what's waiting inside for me. I catch up to her before she walks inside alone. My men shoot first, ask second, which is proper. I know the two at the other warehouse were just shocked and probably did pull guns on her, but didn't fire after she started talking.

***

Ten minutes in and they have gone back to being tight lipped. I'm about to call it. "Would you three mind getting me an unopened bottle of water?" I should have asked if she needed anything before I got started. I need to find a chick and fuck her so I get this one out of my head. They run off without a look at me. Usually, they are like lost puppies.

"Go ahead. See if you can find out this stuff." I hand her a piece of paper. I like a reminder of the reason for the interrogation because I have lost myself to the thrill of torture. This way, I bring myself back to the main reasons.

"Hi. Do you mind if I talk to you guys?" Like they are going to mind. This is going to be the most unorthodox thing I've seen in a warehouse in a while. "Great, thanks. Why don't we just get to know each other? I'm Dani, a consultant, typically in the accounting field, but I do branch out to other fields when I can. Multiple college degrees and professional designations. But, what I truly love is my pet squirrel. He has a picnic bench where I leave peanuts for him, which he loves. Great squirrel really. What about you?"

"Uh, I'm Aldo." She nods like he's saying the most important thing in the world. "I've worked for his dad since I was a teenager."

"Hi Aldo, it's nice to meet you. If you work for his dad, they must have the wrong person. What do they think you did?" She has the answer on the sheet I gave her. I'm about to go ask if she can read when she puts her hand behind her and does some signal. Whatever that means.

"They think we sold secrets." She just gives him a look and he keeps going. "I might have had some debt with Marino and he said if I could bring him information about the Segreto family, they would be erased. I like to gamble and the information wasn't dangerous."

"Well, what information and who gave it to you? If it's what you are saying Aldo, I'm sure it's just a misunderstanding."

It's not just a misunderstanding, he sold a lot of information to Marino and now we have to either kill all of them or make the information useless, which is why we are having this chat. "Locations of buildings, number of people there, and some little things. Frankie gave it to us. All it took was a six pack." At least I know who to bring in next.

"Let me guess, it started with the little things and then the requests kept getting bigger and now you are giving too many locations to Marino?" She asks it in such a calm, understanding demeanor that I'm ready to give her answers. I think she should teach the guys interview skills. Aldo nods. "Can you remember the locations?" Another nod. "Great, I'm going to write them down as you say them so they know you're being helpful."

Aldo lists three locations which aren't anything special. They are all by the docks and we can easily switch docks to make the information useless. As I'm getting a plan together, I look back to the scene unfolding. "Anything else weighing on you, Aldo? You can tell me, we're friends."

"Well, there is one other thing. You see, the Marino family wanted locations of where Matteo goes on dates and for dinner, which we gave them. But we heard someone from that family killed Matteo's friend. Then, we were told that it wasn't a friend, but it was his boyfriend." Well, shit. That's going to be a problem. We might not care, dad doesn't care, but the family will. Traditions and all that shit.

"That's just a rumor, though, right? Is there any proof?" She asks with an ease that I wonder how many times she's done this before.

Tim finally speaks. "No proof, but why would someone lie?"

"Many reasons. I'm sure in this world many don't care, but in the families, they don't want traditions spat on." I'm surprised she knows that. "But a rumor, well, that might cause two families to fight and open up real estate or financial gains for the other families. Good news. I know this friend. Not through Matteo, and he was as straight as an arrow. He loved going to weird locations that seem random, especially this diner that had a clock on the outside. Open 24/7, great burgers and shakes."

"Oh. If you know about the diner, it must be the same guy." Aldo bought that too easily. Maybe it'll be a blessing to take him out.

"Anything else to add Tim?" He shakes his head. I knew we wouldn't get a lot out of him. He's always been quiet. "Aldo?" He looks down. "Is there something else?" She says it so softly that I doubt Tim, who is right there, heard her.

"There is one other thing."

"Don't say another word Aldo, I mean it."

"Aldo, don't listen to Tim, we're friends here. It will just stay in this room." Aldo doesn't take the bait. She turns around and grabs tape and headphones. "Now that Tim can't hear us, what was that other thing?"

Aldo actually looks terrified. "So, the friend that was killed." He waits until she nods. "There is another hit on the market. For his sister. Hundred grand. The problem is nobody knows her real name. Apparently, she's always changing it, moving around. Nobody can find her."

"Do you know who put the hit on her?" Aldo misses that her hands are now shaking. I need to step in and get her out of here, but if we know who, I can keep her safe.

"The Irish." He whispers like that will keep him safer.

"Thank you for the information, Aldo. You were extremely helpful." She gives him a huge smile. I don't know how since she just found out she has a hit on her head. "I'm going to go now and leave you with these men. I have work in the morning." Without another word, she walks away from Aldo and Tim, who are now screaming. Well, Tim is trying to with the tape over his mouth.

She walks straight to my car and climbs inside. "Thank you." She just nods after I say the two words that are almost foreign to me.

I start driving to her hotel, but when I get a block away from my place, I turn and see that she's asleep. I can't leave her alone in a hotel. Too many people have access and there is nobody there to watch her back. I make a quick decision and park in the underground lot and take the elevator to my penthouse.

After carrying her inside, I place her in the guest room bed and tuck her in. I grab a bottle of water and leave it on the nightstand. Finally, I plug her phone into the extra charger before turning out the lights and closing the door.

I text my dad to make sure everything was handled and let him know that we will be in late this morning. It's already 3. I'm about to get in the shower when my phone rings. My dad never calls. "Everything ok?"

"Why is there a hit out on this consultant? And why did you bring her to another warehouse to assist in an interrogation?" Great, a sleep-deprived father is never good.

"I don't know, but I plan to find out. She got the information we needed. I'll fill you in later. Night." All I get is a grunt before the call ends.

Chapter 5

Daniella

I wake with a start. What time is it? Where am I? All I remember is leaving a warehouse and getting into a car. I know this isn't my hotel room. It's far too nice. Don't get me wrong the Four Seasons is magical, but this is, without a doubt, a guest room in some fancy house.

I get out of bed and search for my shoes, phone, and bag. I find two, but not my bag. Then the events of last night, early morning, come rushing back. I tortured four guys. In front of my client. Today is going to be a long one. I still don't know whose house I'm in though.

I somehow find my way to the door, which is an elevator and call an Uber. At least they know my location even if I don't. I get dropped off across the street from the hotel, never give someone your actual location, and get up to my room. At least it's still early enough that I can shower, change, eat a quick breakfast, and get to work before 9.

My shower takes the longest, but I'm back in the lobby before I realize that I don't have a car anymore. It's not far to walk to that office, but it's still winter. Oh well. I leave and start the walk only to be stopped by a blacked-out SUV. Don't get in the car no matter what they offer you or how attractive the driver is. I walk the opposite direction since they won't be able to flip around. I can circle back. I'm not the best with directions, but New York is just a giant grid. I hope.

I don't get to find out. A man in a suit, too expensive of a suit, stops me. "He's already grumpy that you left without a note or saying anything." Well, that's just great. I don't know who 'he' is. Either hes.

"Not my problem." I go to walk around him, but he just slides in front of me. How do people his size move that easily. I won't out run him and my stun gun is in my missing bag. Huffing out a breath, I stomp to the SUV and get in. Yes, I know. This could be the person with a hit on me, but unless I wanted to play in traffic, this was the only choice. I thought New Jersey drivers were aggressive, but city drivers are worse.

"I brought coffee. Also, you won't be returning to your hotel room." I find Tony looking straight at me as I climb into the passenger seat.

"I won't be? Who decides where I sleep? I thought it was me. I'm not dragging anyone into the mess with the Irish, so you can forget about me staying with you." I cross my arms only to lose my stance a moment later when the smell of the coffee reaches me. "Thanks." I say hopefully quiet enough that he doesn't hear.

He pulls into traffic with the patience of a saint, even though we both know he isn't. "Well, you have choices of where to stay. My place, which is the best offer. My father's estate, which is terrifying. Or with Matteo, but he is not only mourning the loss of your brother, but is staying at your brother's place." Almost like a lightbulb went off in his head, he looks at me when we stop at the light. "Why aren't you staying at your brother's?"

I know we didn't get much sleep, but I thought he had some brains. "You mean so people who are trying to kill me can easily find me? Because who has access to my brother's place that is a female?"

"Wouldn't your mother?" He is actually curious. "Not that you could be mistaken as your mother." He cringes a little when he realizes how bad it might have been.

"She's dead. Most likely killed by the same people that want me dead, too." I look out the windshield. This isn't a conversation I ever want to have but at least he isn't looking at me with pity. "You didn't figure that out when you did your background investigation on me?" I'm back to questioning his skills and intelligence. Unless he usually doesn't do the checks.

"I found you and your brother. When I saw your brother, I got distracted since I met him with Matteo. I was curious it you'd tell me the truth." He trails off like he might regret saying something else.

I know the look on his face all too well. He wants to take his brother's pain, but he can't. Nobody can. Unless he lets someone in to help, but I don't expect that to happen right away. "Do you know where my bag is? I had it in my car, which your guys stole. Also, is your brother going to be in the office today?"

That gets me a glance. Good, he didn't learn that I can be extremely scatter-brained, but I usually do it so I don't have to keep discussing hard topics. "Your bag is in the back seat. It was checked for listening and tracking devices, but everything is still in there. He should be."

***

After finishing the drive and ascent to the office in silence, I take out the letter from my bag and go in search of Matteo's office. I find him sitting with his back to the door in what looks like the same clothing from last night.

"Knock, knock." I say lightly as I knock on his door.

"I thought you and my brother weren't coming in today. At least that's what dad said."

I know he doesn't want me to ask, but. "They're both dead, right?" He nods. Almost like he thinks I'll look at him any differently. "Good. This is yours." I leave the envelope on a small box that I promised to give him if my brother couldn't.

As I'm walking out, I hear him pick up both items. I close the door. He's going to need privacy for all his emotions. Especially once he realizes it was an engagement ring my brother left him. On my way back to my office, I let myself wonder how amazing they would have been for each other.

Once I sit at my desk, I let myself get lost in work. Which is what I've been doing since my brother died. With work, there are no emotions. Nobody is actively trying to kill me at my desk. Nobody is giving me puppy eyes because my parents and brother were killed. At least only a few know I'm next.

I'm jarred from my thoughts, thinking I might have found my first real lead, when I hear a knock. Before I can say anything, the door swings open. "I brought lunch." As I'm about to decline, my stomach makes it known that I'm actually starving. "Good. You're hungry."

Matteo puts the bag of food on the small table by the couch. Yes, this office has a couch, why, no clue. Maybe I can just stay here instead of with one of the Segreto family members. "You didn't have to do this. But I am very thankful you did."

"Actually, I did. Your brother left me specific instructions. You don't eat when you get invested in a case. Somehow, you forget. I also know that last night you probably only got four hours of sleep after you left the warehouse."

"Two, at most, actually." I say around a bite of my sandwich.

That stops him with his sub halfway to his mouth. "Two? You left when I started."

"We were on our way to my hotel, but your brother got a call with his assignment. When we got there, they decided to stop talking. Not that they were before hand, but they said they would if he came. So, I had a little more work last night. Then your brother kidnapped me and took me to his place. I got a ride back to my place before trying to come in this morning."

"You slept at Tony's place?" I nod. I thought that part was clear. Who knows, but this sandwich is delicious. Then I realize I haven't eaten all day. So, my gauge is possibly off. "What did his assignment say?"

"Nope. That's a question for him, not me. I got the information out. What he does with it is up to you or him or your father." He seems to like this answer because he returns to attacking his lunch. I know I get hungry, but he looks like he hasn't eaten in a while. The letter probably scolded him about not forgetting to eat himself. Alex has always been the nurturing type. It just got worse after our parents died.

We eat the rest of our meal in silence. I don't miss the ring he is now wearing. On his right hand instead of his left. Nobody needs to know why or where it came from, but it fits him perfectly. Before I start crying, I start cleaning up. A busy mind should help keep the emotions at bay.

"I would've said yes." At least he shut the door when he entered because that breaks me. All the tears come rushing out. He lets me have all the time I need as I soak his shirt.

Once I've cleaned up and composed myself, I let the words I've been dying to say since I first saw him after everything. "I remember when he first met you. He swore he found his person. Then, I met you and knew he did. You were so uncomfortable at first, but the entire time, you made such an effort because you knew it was important for him. Then he called me after meeting Tony. He knew who your family was, but he wanted you even if it wasn't out in the open. He was prepared to make all the sacrifices to keep you safe. He bought the ring a week before he was killed. He was going to propose after this dinner he set up."

Now his face is covered in tears. "I went to that dinner and thought he stood me up. I was so upset. I knew something was off because I bought him this for that night." He pulls out a similar ring to the one he's wearing. "I just couldn't figure out what was wrong. The obituary was hidden. There were no investigations or autopsies matching his description. I figured he got scared and ran, even though I knew he would never leave me if he could help it."

We end up sitting next to each other wondering about the wedding and their future together. I don't know how long it was but his phone ringing snapped us out of it. "I'm sorry. I have to take this." Without another word, he leaves my office.

***

The rest of the day goes by without any more interruptions. I've asked the accounting people who gives them procedures to follow and other questions. Everything keeps coming back to one person. Hal.

You would think people committing fraud would be smarter. Especially, this intricate of a scheme. It should have a smart mastermind behind it. Everything leads back to him though. The only companies not impacted are the ones he is in charge of. He's telling people to add money onto invoices for overhead. All small amounts, but it adds up.

I'll need a few more days to get all the data needed to not only verify but get an amount. I just don't know how Mr. Segreto is going to take being told his best friend is behind this.

As I'm packing up for the day, I see three figures standing in the doorway. I've been staring at screens so I can't make them out. There is no way I'm getting around them, so I might as well not panic?

My eyes finally adjust when the last one files into the office and closes the door. "Who are you staying with." The words say question, but it's more of a demand. There is no choice, but to answer. They aren't going to like what I have to say. I'm also fairly certain nobody says no to the boss.

"Myself. In my hotel room." As I pull the bag over my shoulder, I see their mouths open. "Alone." I don't need violence or threats here, but I don't think I'm going to get my way.

"Alright. How do you want to get there?" He asks like I have a choice, but I'm sure someone is going to be thrilled when I say taxi.

"She can take an Uber like she did from my place this morning, dad. That way the person threatening to kill her can track her." Yeah, sarcasm.

I go for the knock out. If they can't see the reason, I guess it has to be spoon fed. Let's just hope Matteo came out to his father already. He wasn't out when he was with Alex. "That's a wonderful idea. Why don't I just put all three of you in more harm's way by staying with you and being in your car. Nobody knows my name, but I'm sure nobody gossips in a mafia. I'm sure nobody will figure out that I changed my name. Nobody will discover I know a certain person that was killed. You're right. Which one of you would like to be targeted more than you already are? Can you assure my safety?"

When nobody answers, I take that as an answer and walk past them out the door and into the elevator. I think I'm actually going to get away with this when the elevator doesn't move. The doors closed. I pressed the button for lobby. The elevator did that shake thing it does right before it starts moving, but it's not moving.

Great. I was prepared for an assassin attempting to kill me. Crazy people on bikes maybe. Hell, even poison in my food. I was not prepared for the elevator and my own panic to be my downfall. I don't like elevators. I don't like small spaces. Usually, I can handle myself, but I did just yell at a leader of a mafia family plus threaten his two sons. Him I could see killing me.

That'd be fine. This is not fine.

I try all my relaxation techniques. Box-breathing. Imagine you're on a cloud. Counting. Anything to not think about being stuck in an elevator. Nothing is working. I resort to the one thing I excel at that would actually be helpful in this situation.

I scream bloody murder. If someone is trying to pull a prank, they'll get ruptured eardrums. I do not take lightly to being locked away somewhere. If the boss thinks I'll roll over after this, he has another thing coming. I'll just sleep on that couch. It was comfortable enough. I don't have clothes, but that's not my problem.

Chapter 6

Tony

Waking up to a notification that my penthouse door was opened, aka the elevator was called, I tried to stop her. There is no way I'm letting her out by herself after learning there is a hit on her. She's gone before I can stop her, so I make the decision to wait outside her hotel. After getting her to the office, I need space. There is no good reason to not allow me to assist her. Keep her safe. That's all I want. Her safe. Preferably in my bed, no guest room, but baby steps.

First stop is my dad's office. I told my dad what happened last night since I just gave him the highlights briefly. All of it. He agrees that she needs to stay with one of us. He also knows that my place is the realistic choice. Matteo is not in the right headspace to watch over her. I let him deal with her all day though. I actually get everything finished.

My dad collects Matteo and I to confront her about where she is staying. I've never seen anyone tell my father no and walk right past him. I shouldn't be as turned on as I am right now, but damn.

We watch her enter the elevator. My dad has the stop button ready to be pressed as the doors close. I figure this is to make a point and they will reopen right away. But after a few minutes, I look at Matteo, he had the same thought I did. However, he knows her better through Alex. We wait another minute.

"Uh, dad, she has anxiety with small spaces. I don't think this will win her over." Anytime one of us tells my dad something controversial, we both hold our breath.

"I'm sure…" Whatever he was about finish his sentence with is cut off by screams. We've dealt with screamers in the past. It's common when people are tortured, but these are heartbreaking. They cut through all of us. "Shit. Shit. Shit." He keeps talking as he is releasing the elevator from his hold. The doors open after a few seconds and she pushes past us.

Great. Now, we have an anxious girl with weapons in her bag facing us down. None of us have experience with anxiety or how to treat someone with it in the last decade. Well, I used to have panic attacks, but when I was brought into the warehouse scene, it stopped. My dad is frozen, which never happens. He always has a plan. Hell, probably the entire alphabet full of plan options.

My brother is also frozen, but for a different reason. He knows the one person that would have been the best person to ask is dead.

I pull my phone out and dial the doctor on retainer. "Doc, how do we calm someone down while they are having a panic attack?"

"Anxiety? Nobody's bleeding out? Right, what caused the panic attack?"

"Locked in an elevator. She apparently doesn't like small spaces." Hopefully that helps him, but it sounds like he'd rather have one of us shot.

A long pause and the sound of flipping pages. This is throwing everyone. "You don't have anti-anxiety drugs because that would have been step one." He must be thinking out loud. "She's out of the elevator. Keep her in a wide-open space with windows. That should help. I can grab some medicine that should calm her down?" I think he should know what to do and not be asking me. "Where are you?"

"Mid-town office. I'll let them know downstairs to express you up." After that, I hang up. Eyes are still on her, but I don't think she realizes we are all in the same room. I send a text to security to expect him. I should have asked if we should try talking to her.

Here goes anything. Maybe this will win me points. "Daniella? It's Tony. Would you like some water?" I act like I'm approaching a scared kid or a puppy. She can see my hands and the water bottle I grabbed. If doc is bringing drugs, I don't want to mix alcohol into the equation.

She takes the bottle without hesitation, but I offer to open it since her hands are still shaking. "I'm going to sleep on the couch." The words come out barely audible. She stands and starts stripping on the way to the office we have her in.

I turn to look at my family because if this is normal, I need to know how many people have seen her naked. And how to prevent this from happening ever again because she's mine. Both of them have their eyes closed. "Tony!" my dad hisses. I stop staring after her and look back to them. They are both staring at me like I've lost my mind. I have. I've never wanted a person as much as her. She's pulled me in without even kissing me yet.

"Matteo, you get her some clothes from Alex's place. Bring all of us a change of clothes for tomorrow. If she insists on spending the night on that couch, we'll be staying here. Then, move her stuff from her hotel room into Tony's spare bedroom. After you drop the stuff off, you can sleep wherever. Actually, move her stuff tomorrow. It's been a long 36 hours for you." He gives the orders and heads towards his office. We both know he has a bed hidden in his office, but I wasn't expecting him to stay here. We have security downstairs.

I look at my brother who is still frozen. He has a key to my place and he knows where she is staying so I don't know why he isn't gone yet. "I've got her. Get some sleep. Nobody is getting up here without permission. Don't worry." He nods and I push the elevator button so he leaves.

Without another word, he gets in the elevator as the doc exits. I nod to the doctor and he follows me to her office. I knock and wait until I hear confirmation before I open the door. "This is the family doctor. I'll be out here if you need me." I go to sit at the closest desk, but I don't have a chance because the doctor is already coming back out. "That was quick."

"She's refusing to let me check her out. She doesn't want any medicines. So here." He passes a blank bottle full of pills to me. "If this ever happens again, which I hope it doesn't, break up one of these and give it to her. She is most likely going to crash on that couch, but it's going to take a little for her to calm down enough to sleep. I don't know what caused her panic, but it's definitely something traumatic." He goes to leave, but I see him stop at my dad's office.

I guess it's going to be another long night. I knock and poke my head into her office. "I'm going to be in my office if you need anything."

***

I haven't gotten a single minute of sleep. I always sleep after working myself in the warehouses, but watching her yesterday deal with everyone then having her under my roof, I didn't sleep. Add on knowing someone put a hit on her and not knowing why. Yeah, there was no chance I was sleeping last night.

Tonight though, I should have slept easier. We have security downstairs. Nobody knows were here. My dad is also here, so I'd have backup.

Hearing someone open the cabinets and running water, I jump off the couch and grab my gun. My dad doesn't get up in the middle of the night unless he gets a call. Out of my office, I see my dad had the same idea. I circle around so we can stop the intruder.

I watch my dad lower his gun before I see into the kitchen. "Do you guys want me to grab anything for you?" She doesn't even turnaround from the toaster. "You have strawberry pop tarts, which is exciting. Should I start a pot of coffee or do you not want a cup?" She grabs them out of the toaster and faces us.

She looks like she hasn't slept, but she can't be that awake at all. My father grunts. "I guess he's going back to sleep. We need to talk later this morning, sir. Not only about last night, but I almost have the total that was stolen."

I know I'm sleep deprived but how did she learn his grunts that fast? "I'll take both pop tarts and coffee, but no need for a full pot now." I go grab a pack and pop them in the toaster before I grab a mug and pod for coffee. "How did you sleep?"

"Oh, I haven't. I never sleep. Why do you have pop tarts? I get the other stuff, but it seems like you keep it fairly healthy." I get not talking about what happened, but I'm going to need answers before the day is over.

"Matteo. Plus, the men in the organization work weird hours. We like to make sure there are some good midnight snacks available. It's also why we have beds in all the offices." I watch her while we eat breakfast. "Why are you so against staying with one of us?" I know the elevator is off limits, but if I can understand her motivation for leaving and pissing off the head of the family, maybe I can talk to my dad before he loses it on her.

She finishes her breakfast before speaking. "I don't need more people's death on my hands." She walks back to her office and slams the door shut. I want to see who is more stubborn, her or my dad. Nobody has ever squared off against him and won, but I think I found out who would.

All I know right now, it's going to be a long day.

***

As soon as Matteo arrives with a clean set of clothes for all of us, I shower and go to his office. Without sleeping, I got all the work I needed to done for today before it even started. There is something nice about working during the middle of the night. Nobody expects anything from you. You can stare at a wall for an hour and nobody will judge you.

Knocking on his door, I walk in and sit across from him. I closed the door on my way in, so his secret would remain his. "How did you know about Daniella's issues with small spaces?" It's been one of the many things I haven't stopped thinking about all night.

"Alex was the same way. Apparently, the night their parents were killed, they locked them in panic rooms separately. We worked together so he could handle being in an elevator, but he still preferred taking the stairs. I figured if he was that bad, she would have been worse since she was a few years younger." He hasn't talked about him since he found out.

"What changed?" Since our mom left, we have been able to read each other and talk without words. That's what happens when your only parent throws themselves into work so they don't deal with losing a spouse.

He holds up a letter and a box. "She gave me this. Apparently, he was going to propose the day after he was killed. Left me the ring and everything. He also asked that I protect her, which is going to be more difficult than I originally thought." He has the same breakfast he always has. "Why are you trying so hard to get her to stay with you? We have the Four Seasons in our pocket, nobody will get to her."

How do I explain to him that she has me hooked and I haven't even kissed her yet? Every time I think I have a hold of myself, she pulls me back to her. I can't walk away. I tried to pick up some random girl after the first time I saw her and I couldn't because nobody compared.

"Oh no. I know that look. Do you think it's a good idea to get involved? She already has a hit on her. Do you want to be the reason she gets hurt or worse?"

"I don't know what I'm doing here. You know me. I don't do relationships. I don't want to end up like dad. I don't want to go through what you're dealing with either though. I just can't explain it." I pour myself a drink from his wet bar. Another random thing most offices have. You never know when you'll need a drink.

"She doesn't do relationships, either." He whispers.

I don't know what to think about that. She's beautiful. "Why not? She's gorgeous and intelligent." The men in this city are idiots if they passed her over.

I feel like he knows something I don't. "She doesn't want to fall for someone and then end up dead like her brother. She lost her parents and now her brother. She was trained to handle herself. She wasn't taught how to let someone in." That brings up the other night.

"Who taught her how to torture? Because that was something else." I can't tell him exactly how that made me feel unless I never want to hear the end of it.

He opens his mouth, but quickly closes it. "That's not my story to tell. I've already said more than I should have." Knowing he won't give me any more information, I head back to my office. I'm going to need to get some sleep before tonight. When I get to the door, I realize I forgot to ask about her clothes. "They are in your spare bedroom closet. The nice one."

On my way to my office, I notice my dad's office door is shut. However, everyone is looking at the door where loud voices are coming from. The only benefit is nobody can understand the words. I look at Daniella's office door, which is open. It must be her inside. I glare at everyone I pass so they stop trying to listen in.

I knock on his door. "What!"

Oh, this is going to be bad. I quickly enter and shut the door behind me. I'm not shocked Daniella is inside. I am shocked she is getting away with yelling at him though. "Just so you both are aware, the walls are apparently thinner than we thought and your voices travel. Either calm down and talk like normal humans or I'm going to have to ask you both to wait until you are able to do that."

Chapter 7

Daniella

After last night, I knew this conversation was coming. I can't believe they thought locking me in an elevator was the right decision. I know my brother told Matteo about small spaces and his hatred for them. He didn't tell his father or brother, there was no point. But once he saw what his father did, I would have expected him to step in.

I don't knock, I just slam Mr. Segreto's office door shut. I don't care if he shoots me. We are going to deal with this before I try to leave again. I will not be put into another anxiety spiral. It's not going to be pretty, but I don't care. I refuse to let anyone treat me like that. I'm not going down without a fight and he will not like trying to fight me.

My brother always told me I had a temper and my mouth would get me into trouble one day. I don't think he thought it would be the hands of his future father-in-law. "We're going to discuss last night right now. I don't want to put either you or your sons in harm's way, which is *exactly* what you will do if you force me to stay with one of you. I know there is a hit on me. I know I will die soon, but that's ok. I don't want to put my death on your shoulders. It's not your responsibility now or ever to make sure I don't end up dead. I know you aren't used to people telling you no, but I need you to let me go when it's my time."

I'm surprised my voice is as firm as it is when I tell him all this. I'm more surprised he let me get it all out. I know he probably has a lot to respond with, but I can't help my sigh of relief when he puts the gun that was in his hand down.

"Sure, enter my office and tell me what's going to happen right now." Maybe I should have waited until we both got sleep before. "You put all of us in harm's way when my son fell in love with your brother? I don't think that was your fault, but if you were involved in that, thank you."

Not sure I am breathing, but I thought he didn't know Matteo was dating my brother. "He came about a week before he was killed. He asked permission to marry my son. Luckily, he knew not to say anything in front of anyone else. When he asked, I knew my son was getting a good one. I was waiting for him to tell me, but I've known for years."

Of course, he would ask permission. He was always following traditions. "I knew he was planning to propose, but I didn't know about your meeting with him. When I met Matteo, I knew they were each other's person. Now, I just hope he finds someone to keep him happy. That's what Alex would have wanted."

I see the happiness in Mr. Segreto's face that his son was loved so much. "Alright. Why don't we have a family dinner tonight and I can safely explain why you should stay with Tony? I would feel better knowing someone was watching your back. I know Matteo would feel better too, since I'm sure your brother asked him to keep an eye on you."

That's exactly what he would have done. It's not fair to put my survival on them. I say the only thing that might change his mind, but I feel even this won't change it. "I don't want either of your sons to know this." I wait until he nods. "I'm the reason my parents and my brother were killed. They want me. My family was trying to keep me safe, but if they just got me instead, my family would still be alive." I hope the walls don't have ears. I haven't spoken those words since my parents died when I told my brother.

"Why do you think you were the reason?" With how softly we are both talking, I bet people don't know we are both in here.

"I got into a small fight and ended up beating a kid who is Irish. He wasn't supposed to lose a fight. I knew better than fighting, but he threw the first punch. I ended it." I never gave the truth to Alex. He didn't need to carry around the guilt. "That kid, well, he is now the underboss."

"I thought you were from Jersey."

"My dad did a lot of work in the city."

He sits back in his chair and observes me. "There is no way a family put a hundred grand on your head for a fight as a child. Until I figure out who and why this hit was put on you, I need you to stay with Tony. That way, you can keep an eye on him and vice versa. So, dinner tonight. No dairy."

"Deal. We can discuss my findings then since it will just be the four of us."

He nods but stands up. "Come sit over here. After last night and this talk, I need a break." I have no clue what he plans to do, but I go over and sit next to him on the couch, leaving a full seat between us. He pushes a button and a tv comes out of the table and he passes me a controller.

"Mario Kart?" I know the theme song before the video even shows.

"It's the best stress reliever. Well, best legal one. I know you didn't sleep last night after, well. Plus, the past few days have been stressful, so why not have a little fun."

***

We're on the ninth race. This is the tie breaker when a knock sounds, I almost break focus when Mr. Segreto yells enter.

His son enters and just starts scolding us. "Just so you both are aware; the walls are apparently thin and your voices travel. Either calm down and talk like normal humans or I'm going to have to ask you both to wait until are able to do that."

His words don't make sense. We weren't loud. Alright, maybe we were cursing and talking smack, but nothing bad. I don't think either of us has been this calm since we met. Mr. Segreto pauses the game, takes my controller, and frowns. "Fine, but we are going to need a rematch to break the tie." I nod in agreement.

Tony finally takes in the scene. "What the hell?" I think it's more to himself than us, but I answer anyway. I'm helpful like that.

"Your father invited me over for dinner tonight. We agreed that I will stay with you while completing my investigation here and you will assist me with the investigation into who wants me dead. Oh, it's just the four of us tonight, so we will need to let Matteo know." I specifically left out the part he was actually asking about. There is no need for him to know I love racing games. I let his dad win a few, so I would get invited back. "Also, don't fuck with the elevators ever again."

I nod to Mr. Segreto and head back to my office. Everyone is staring at me. Once I'm back at my desk, I take in my outfit. Nothing is spilled on it; my hair isn't too crazy. I don't know what they were staring at.

***

By lunch, I'm starting to waver. Maybe I shouldn't have accepted dinner tonight. I don't think I'll make it that long, but if I sleep now, I won't sleep later. It's almost like my thoughts drew him to my office. "Want to head back to my place before dinner tonight? I think we put in enough hours today and yesterday."

I'm not excited to be going back to his place, but I am excited to leave. I pack up my notes and all the stuff Matteo brought in this morning. As soon as the elevator arrives, my panic from last night returns. I didn't think this through. The amount of time it would take me to get to the lobby from this floor would be later than dinner. I also don't have the energy for that.

We get to the lobby quickly. Apparently, Tony has an override card that allows us to have express service. "Can we stop at the hotel so I can grab my stuff?" I think this is reasonable, but he doesn't say anything until we get into the car and it starts moving.

"There's no need."

Interesting. I can think of a few reasons. Clothes, toiletries, not paying for a room I'm not using, snacks. I have a lot of snacks in that room. "Why not?" There are a lot of things I'm learning about these men, one being they hate being questioned. That might be all men though.

"Matteo went this morning, gathered all your stuff, and checked out." He says it like it's just a regular Tuesday. Talk about invasion of privacy. When I look down at my outfit, I know I didn't have it in my hotel room. "He also packed your stuff from your brother's place and brought it over."

I should have fought harder against staying with him. This is going to be a disaster. They clearly are not used to the word no and that is one of my favorite words. On the rest of the drive, I try to figure out a good plan to deal with getting out of living with Tony, but I think I finally found someone more stubborn than me. His father.

Once we get into his apartment, I actually take it all in. The first time I was carried inside and then escaped out of in the early morning. "Would you like a tour since you didn't get one last time?"

Just because of that, I don't want one. "How do you know I didn't investigate before I left?"

He smirks. I don't know if I'm going to be able to sleep here and not end up in his bed. If I sleep with him, he will end up like his brother, pinning after someone who is dead. "Last time you were here, you poked your head out of the door. Looked up and down the hallway. Found the front door and bolted. I know because there are cameras in all the common areas. Nothing in bedrooms or bathrooms because that would be weird."

Right. It is completely normal to have your entire house taped. The more I think about it, the more it makes sense in a weird way. He is literally the son of a crime lord. I would assume he has people actively trying to kill him on a daily basis. He'd want to know when someone was in his home. It doesn't feel like a home though. There are no personal effects. If I didn't know this was his place, I don't think I'd be able to figure it out.

"Why does it seem like nobody lives here?" Nothing is out of place and it is extremely clean for a single bachelor. At least from what I hear. I make a point not to get involved with bachelors. Or anyone at all. No point in breaking someone's heart when I know I'll be gone before I can have the life I actually want.

He looks around like I just insulted him. "It wasn't an insult. The place looks like a photoshoot for luxury living."

He just blinks, no emotion. All the other times I've been with him, he's shown his emotions. Now, I wonder if he's trying to hide something from me. He starts the tour, but leaves out his bedroom. Why am I wondering where he sleeps? That's not good. I've never been interested in getting to know someone romantically, but ever since I laid eyes on Tony, I wonder if he'd be a good father. Does he even want kids? Do I want kids? Does he want a big wedding? After my parents, I decided a simple ceremony would be perfect. Nothing too big or flashy with Alex walking me down the aisle. Without him, I don't know if I'll ever get to meet my person though.

I didn't even realize we finished the tour, but when I look over, I see him smirking. "What were you thinking about?" I feel my face heat up. There is no way he knows where my mind went to. "It's even better than I thought it was going to be."

He truly knows how to stroke my emotions; brings them all out of me. Now, it's anger. "How would you know what I was thinking?"

Instead of the smirk, I'm graced with his full smile. There goes my anger. He can't look that good smiling. "Well, you were flush and when I asked you, you immediately blushed. Then your pulse picked up. I've been around enough women to know when they are thinking about me. Typically, it's something fun, but with you, I don't know what it is. I never get hung up on a woman, but you seem to have ruined them all for me and I haven't even kissed you yet. I know you aren't ready for that and I can be patient, but it's not going to last long with you and I under the same roof."

"I'm going to die soon; do you really want to feel like your bother does right now?" I don't address everything else because I would gladly throw caution to the wind and jump his bones. I can risk my heart, but for some reason, I can't risk his.

"Is that the only thing stopping you?" I knew he wouldn't answer my question, but I don't think I can give him what he wants yet. After dinner tonight, his father might actually be the one who accomplishes killing me.

"Seriously? Your father is most likely going to kill me tonight when I break the news to him that his best friend. The man he grew up with and has been by his side has stolen a lot from him. There is also your brother who was going to marry my brother had he not died and now he feels he has to keep me alive. So, no that's not the only reason. I don't need your family hating me more for hurting you." I go back to the kitchen. I don't need to sit in the living room and listen to him.

"I don't think that's your decision alone to make. How do you know I won't feel that way regardless of if we get involved?" He makes this announcement after following me. I get that this is his home, but I could really like some time alone. "You're in my head. I haven't been able to get you out since that first day. So as much as I'd love to find another girl and fuck her, I haven't been able to since none of them compare to you. You see, you will be mine."

Chapter 8

Tony

I've never danced around a subject. She really doesn't understand. I just want her and she wants to fight me at every turn. At least, she didn't deny that she is attracted to me. I'm worried about tonight now. I don't think my dad will kill her after he found someone he can beat in Mario Kart.

"We have about an hour before we have to leave for my dad's. If you want to rest or change or whatever, you can. I'm going to the gym." I need to get out of here before I do or say something. I need to be on at dinner if I have any hope of sleeping tonight.

I get almost into my room when I hear her footsteps. "Where's the gym? Is it downstairs?"

I left my bedroom and the gym off the tour so I would have some place without thinking about her in there. "It's at the end of the hallway." That's all I say. I need to work out all these emotions.

After changing, I blast my headphones and open the door. I freeze. She's running on the treadmill with her back to me. I try to ignore her and go to the weights. I was planning to run as well, but not now.

Twenty minutes later, she finally leaves. Thankfully, I'm able to run because the weights weren't doing enough. After running for twenty minutes, I realize I need to stop so I have time to shower before dinner.

All dressed, I head into the living room, but Daniella is already there pacing. She dressed up. I have seen her for work, but this is something else. If I didn't realize how beautiful she was, it would have concerned me. "Ready?" She just nods. What is there to say anyway? I knew she'd be nervous, but I'm just hoping she doesn't start panicking. The doctor gave me the medicine, but he didn't walk me through anything else.

Dinner has uneventful. It's all polite conversation and I don't know when the bombs will start. I look at Matteo, he seems to have the same thought process. He's sending me looks like who is stepping between the two if and when things go wrong.

"Boys. Clear the table please." This was always our job. My dad has staff, but he always lets them leave after dinner is made. "Now." I realize he isn't happy about Matteo and I staring at each other since we don't know if we should leave them alone.

As soon as we are away from the table, "Well, are you going to tell me who is stealing?" The good news is we are able to hear everything from the kitchen.

"It's Hal. He's stolen over 1.5 million over the past year. I have all the records and the specific amount at Tony's house. I didn't want to leave any evidence in the office in case someone went snooping." It's so soft like she is trying to keep the accusation out of her tone.

"Did you know?" Matteo whispers.

"Yes, she told me this morning, which is why I've been stressed all day."

He gives me a knowing look. "Right. It has nothing to do with your crush being under the same roof tonight. What did you two do after leaving the office?"

I want to go back into the dining room since the voices are muffled. "I gave her a tour then worked out." That's all I'm going to say, so I go to get more dishes.

"What kind of work out?" I can tell he is smiling and trying not to laugh, but he is following me.

I don't give him an answer even though it's not what he is implying because hopefully tonight it will be the right kind of workout.

The dining room is full of tension. The voices stop as soon as I make it into the room. I grab some more dishes after I saw the daggers my dad was sending our way. As soon as we leave, the voices start again. I don't know why they aren't letting us hear the conversation. My dad doesn't keep anything from us. Especially since Matteo is going to take over soon.

Back in the kitchen, I start loading the dishwasher. "Why aren't we being filled in? Dad keeps us filled in."

Why he's asking me, who knows. "I'm not sure. Maybe they are discussing something else? We need to just wait until one of them tells either of us. Then, we share information with each other." Hopefully, I can get her to tell me tonight in bed. If dad doesn't tell us, we can't ask. It's an unspoken rule. Never question the head of the family. Hell, anyone higher than you in the organization.

"Alex said his sister is more stubborn than a bull. I doubt we'll get any information from either of them until they are ready to share, but we can try."

When we reenter the dining room, I feel Matteo mimic my stiffening. They are hugging? First, Mario Kart, now hugging. I can't even remember the last time either of us were hugged. We just aren't a physically affectionate family.

"Thank you for dinner. It was delicious. I don't remember the last time I had a home-cooked meal that I didn't have to cook." She smiles at my father before saying a quick goodbye to Matteo. I say my goodbyes and we are back in the car.

After pulling out of the driveway, I can't take the silence anymore. "What did my dad have to say?" I try to keep my voice light.

She looks at me from the passenger seat. "If your father wanted you to know, he would have talked in front of you." I thought she would stop talking after that declaration, which I assumed she'd say. "What I can tell you, he was surprised and disappointed, but he believed me. Now, we have a gameplan for everything else I need to get done. There are a few things I'll run by you before presenting them to your dad, which he is aware of. But until I have everything situated and ready, you can't keep asking me. I don't want to lie to you." She turned back to look out the windshield.

I wasn't expecting to get that much, but my dad must have given her an answer for our questions. We drove the rest of the way home in comfortable silence. I call the elevator and we get into the penthouse. Even though I haven't slept the past two nights, I don't want the night to end. "Would you like a nightcap?"

"Sure." Instead of following me into the living room, she goes to the guest room Matteo put her clothes in.

I stay out of her room and pour two drinks. I bring them to the couch and as soon as I sit down, she walks in wearing pajamas. "Thanks for the drink." She takes a sip as she collapses on the couch next to me.

I don't know what to say or do. We're both exhausted, but I can tell she doesn't want this night to end yet. I should just invite her to my room, but I don't think she's there yet. We finish our drinks. "Are you finished?" I nod and she takes the glasses into the kitchen. I follow her.

After putting them into the dishwasher, she comes over to me and I freeze. I never know what she'll do next. "Goodnight." She reaches up on her toes and kisses my cheek before going to her room.

The clock signaling the hour snaps me out of my haze. I head to my bedroom and get into bed.

***

For the first time since I met her, I actually get a good night's sleep. I don't know if it was the kiss on the cheek or something else, but I wake up excited for the day. The smell of bacon also helps. I check the clock and it's 6am. I want to go back to sleep, but the smells are too much. I throw on a pair of pants and go to the kitchen.

I wish I had a camera. I have the video feed, but this needs more something more permanent. She is dancing while cooking. I don't know how much she thinks the two of us will eat since it looks like a diner exploded. There are so many options that I know I don't have to worry about lunch today. She doesn't notice me staring since she must be wearing headphones. I don't want to startle her, but I do. Will she regret the kiss last night? Want more? I go grab a coffee mug so I'm in her eye line.

I duck before the spatula makes contact. "Good morning. How'd you sleep?" I push the buttons so my coffee starts before leaning against the counter.

"Morning." She sounds grumpy, but she's the one up early. "It was fine. You?"

Before I answer, I look at her face. She hasn't slept. "Great. Food smells delicious. Can I help?" I know my cooking skills are nonexistent, but I have to ask. I need to let dad and Matteo know we will not be in today. She needs to rest before she continues down this path. I just need to figure out why she's not sleeping. I'll add it to my ever-growing list.

She faces me with a weird look. "Have you ever cooked?" I stare back. Why would she think that? "I had to take tags off some of the utensils. I'm assuming you have someone cook for you and you just bought the entire kitchen section. Also, you had no food beyond snacks and leftovers. Nobody eats lasagna for breakfast."

Did she leave the apartment without protection again? "How did you get this stuff then?" I'll get to the other questions when I have some food in me.

"The grocery store now delivers. I ordered stuff to be dropped in the lobby and one of your people brought the bags up and left them at the door. No need to worry, I didn't leave again." She turns back to the omelets and flips them onto plates with bacon and potatoes. The fruit is already at the counter.

I wonder if this is how Matteo felt when he met Alex. Did they follow the thought patterns quickly? Were they anticipating questions and concerns? Matteo and I never discussed romantic partners before. One, we never had relationships and *two, we never had relationships*. We had one-night stands. Maybe, one-week stands. That was it. "Thanks for cooking. No, I don't cook. Yes, I have someone to cook for me and grocery shop. I've had lasagna for breakfast." I moan as the cheese from the omelet melts in my mouth. "This is amazing."

We sit and eat in relative silence. I try to stop my moans, but I haven't had a breakfast this good ever. I was never a breakfast eater, but I love breakfast foods. They work any time of day. I finish my plate first and start cleaning up. I need to move or I'll do something stupid like have her for dessert.

"I have to make a call, but don't do the dishes. You cooked, so I'll clean." I go to my room and call my dad. He's usually up by this time.

"Hello." He isn't one for words. He grunts more than talks.

"Dad. Daniella hasn't slept, so I think we should stay in today and come up with a game plan and hopefully, she sleeps a little." I hope he gives me some details of the goal for the game plan because I'm flying blind.

There is a weird pause. He is never at a loss for words; he just doesn't use many. "Why didn't she sleep last night?" Well, that's a new one. He never cared about our love lives. As long as we were careful and didn't make any heirs out of wedlock. That's a big fat no in this family.

"I'm not sure. We had a night cap and we both went into our separate bedrooms. I woke to her cooking breakfast. I'll find out what's actually going on, though, today if we can work from my place." I feel like I'm back in high school.

"Let me know what you figure out. We'll talk on my way home from the office." The line goes dead. I guess we can skip the office.

I go back to the kitchen and she is standing by the sink. "Nope. I will clean. Sit down." I put all the authority possible into my voice and she just rolls her eyes. People usually piss themselves when I use that voice. "We aren't going into the office today. We are going to come up with a game plan."

She just nods. I thought she'd be more something. I can never get a read on her. Sometimes I think she is pissed when she is actually thinking. Others, she is dealing with my father without a care in the world even if her face and voice don't match.

"When is the last time you had a good night sleep?" I focus on the dishes so she doesn't think this is an interrogation.

"Last night." She says it so quickly and firmly, I almost believe her.

"Try again." I order. "Also, just for the record, I hate liars. Do not lie to me. I'd rather be hurt by the truth than comforted with a lie."

"Why does it matter?" I don't answer. "It's been almost a month. How am I supposed to sleep when there is a hit on my head and my family is dead? What's the point?" For the first time, she seems unsure of herself. She's always confident and brave, but right now, with just the two of us, she's scared. Not of being here with me alone, but without her family and knowing anyone could be plotting her death.

I turn the sink off and dry my hands. I got through the pans, but not the plates. "I can have the doctor give you something to sleep. Going without sleep is going to screw you up more than you think." I send a text to the family doctor asking him to stop by. He doesn't need to reply. "As for the hit and family. You are now a part of my family. My father, brother, and I will not let someone kill you. I can't imagine not having a family, but you have to play the cards you were dealt. Would your parents and brother want you to just give up?"

When she doesn't reply, I answer for her. "If you thought that was what you should do, you wouldn't have sought my father out and convinced him to let you look through his books." Now that I say it out loud, how did she convince him?

"I went to your father out of respect for my brother. I don't need to put anyone else, especially my should-have-been in-laws in harm's way." She stomps out of the kitchen and slams her bedroom door shut. This is going to be a fun day.

Chapter 9

Daniella

Walking out of the kitchen was the safest thing I could do. I can't think clearly around him. Is he mad I came into his life? Why would he think my lack of sleeping is causing me to be unable to work? Work is the only thing keeping me going at this point.

If I knew it would work, I'd pick someone to kill me so they can get the money. But then I'd have to deal with two things. The first being facing my parents knowing they wanted me to live on despite everyone dying. The second, which is most likely, not getting to see them after I die. They went up, I'm going down. I didn't learn how torture and kill with fake people. Even if the people were bad and the world is better without them.

I start to relax once I'm in the guest room when the door swings open. "I'm not finished." I was hoping for just a few minutes before I had to face Tony. "Are you planning something I should know about?"

I don't turn to face him. I might not know him well enough, but he's going to see it on my face. I'm no longer living for myself. If I die, no biggie, it's not like I was going to see my family after their funerals.

For a guy his size, I expect to hear him moving, but I feel his fingers gently lift my face so we are looking at each other. "Please." He might not say the words, but he knows what I was thinking by my face. "Whatever you think is the right thing, talk to me first. You are not in this alone anymore."

He whispers like the words might be too much. He was right, they are.

I finally give the words I've known voice. "I'm never going to see them again." Then the tears fall, but instead of being alone, he pulls me into him. Somehow, we end up on the floor with his back against the bed and me in his lap.

It could me minutes or hours, but he lets me get it all out.

***

I don't remember falling asleep. I also can't remember the last time I slept this well and woke up refreshed. When I get my bearings, I have no clue where I am. It's not the guest room Tony set me up in. The blinds aren't closed and its pitch-black outside. I go to get up, but I'm stuck to the bed. I look over my shoulder and Tony is asleep beside me with his arm across my waist and our legs are tangled.

I can't believe I've slept this well when being touched. I have never slept with someone. I am not an after sex cuddler. Not that we had sex, but I have a feeling I'm going to have more questions when we both wake up. Now, how do I get up without waking him?

"I can hear your thoughts, mostriciattola. Lay back down. We can talk in the morning." He grumbles. I can hear the sleep weighing on him. I roll so I'm facing him.

"Tony, get some more sleep." I try to sneak out, but he pulls me closer to his chest.

He opens one eye and then the other. "Why don't you go back to sleep? I don't want to get up."

"You don't have to. Go back to sleep. Don't worry about me. I'm not going anywhere. I just need to get up and move." I lean in and kiss his chest, but that makes him hold me tighter. I can't get any closer, but I'm not going to lie. I haven't been hugged like this since before Alex died.

He rolls me onto him. I can't help but straddle him with my hands falling onto his chest as he groans. "Are you sure you have to get up?" He grinds into me. "We can stay here and not sleep." He moves my hips even as I try to stay still and not give in.

Why does this feel so good? He hasn't even kissed me yet. Why is the night making me feel bolder? Do things I wouldn't necessarily allow? I know he wants me. I can feel how much. I lean down and kiss him. I let myself get lost in this kiss. Even though I started it, he took control immediately. He moves one hand from my hip to tangle in my hair. With him controlling the kiss, I take over moving my hips.

I can't give him everything tonight, but I can make him want more. I missed the feeling of being wanted, something more. I lost myself in the kiss and sensations, but I don't miss him coming and his moans. Even after his orgasm finishes, he keeps kissing me. It's taken on a different feel though, less starved, more cherished.

This time, as I pull away, he lets me. He looks completely relaxed, but he does look like there is unfinished business. I leave the room before I let him even the playing field. I quickly stop in my room to get dressed and brush my teeth.

After I freshen up, I go into the kitchen to make food to eat. I don't know what meal it would be since it's the middle of the night. As I open the fridge, there is no food for me to make with these ingredients. I only ordered necessities for breakfast.

The one good thing about the city, diners are open all day and night. I order a few different items for delivery. I did say I wasn't going to leave, but just going to the lobby shouldn't count.

After fifteen minutes, I go down to the lobby to wait for the food. After paying for the food, I realized I have no way to get back upstairs. I go to the bellhop. He calls up, but there is no answer. I start eating the food and wait until he calls back down. After sorting everything out, I'm back inside to find a much different version of Tony. He's pissed.

"I got food." Holding the bag up as a peace offering. It doesn't seem to work. "Before you say something, I didn't leave the building. I only went to the lobby to pay and get the food."

Instead of relaxing, he actually seems more annoyed. I wait for him to talk, but I'm still hungry. I start setting up the food at the kitchen island. No point setting up at the table since who knows what each of us will eat since we'll probably share a little bit of everything.

He moves into the kitchen in that silent way of his. "I'm pissed because you didn't say anything. I'm not mad that you went downstairs. Why didn't you say something? I would have taken you to get food. You don't need to buy food for me. It's not a good look when others see you pay for us."

That's weird. He knows I have a job that pays fairly well. Why wouldn't I buy us food? "What's wrong with me buying us food? I'm more than capable of paying for food. Also, who would know it wasn't your money?" I pull all the containers to me so he doesn't get any. If he wants to insult me, he can starve.

"You woke me up! I was more than content with staying in bed and eating you. But no, you wanted to get out of bed. You didn't even mention food. For the first time in my life, I've come before the chick I had in bed with me." He grabs a container.

I can't stop my gasp. "That's mine!" I go to grab it back but he dances out of my way and starts eating. "We shouldn't have done anything. It's just going to end with your being heart broken."

He freezes with the burger midway to his open mouth before dropping it back into the container. "It's my heart. I get to say who is and isn't worth risking it for. I want you, which was obvious earlier." He picks the burger back up.

"It is your heart and your choice." I nod as I eat the rest of my first container that I started downstairs. We sit in silence. Using his words from earlier after I'm full. "I can hear your thoughts." As I start cleaning up.

"Why are you so interested in fighting me? I could tell you were into me this morning. One doesn't do what you did without any interest." He pauses as he takes me in like one is trying to figure out the puzzle.

This entire thing is deflating. "I don't want to fight you. I just want to help your father and be done with it all." I don't get what he doesn't understand.

He glares down at me as he rounds the counter to cage me in. "What do mean with be done with it all?" Of course, that is what he focuses on. "Is this related to you not seeing your family again? Why would you assume

60

that?"

His phone starts ringing. It's almost like he knows if he walks away from this conversation, he won't get another chance. "What." He snaps as he answers the phone but he doesn't look away from me. It's almost like he can get all the answers. "Can I call you back? I'm in the middle of something that I need to finish before I do anything else." Well, that answers that question. We aren't finished this line of questioning. Honestly, I'd prefer he torture it out of me. "Thanks, dad. I'll text you when I can talk."

"Nobody will interrupt us. Now, I want to be polite and let you answer all my questions, but I will force them out." I know he's the third highest in the family, but that makes me laugh. He thinks he can actually break me. "What's funny?" He is actually confused.

"You think you can force answers out of me. With what? Torture? If this line of work becomes too much, there's stand-up." I shouldn't laugh. I should be scared as he stalks forward quietly. Like he's locked on his prey. However, he doesn't realize the prey is actually the predator.

"I wasn't going to use torture. There are better, more effective ways of getting information out of woman. For men, torture is the quickest way. They don't like being seen as weak and they have a low tolerance for pain. Women." He shakes his head. "In my line of business, we don't deal with many women and we definitely don't torture them. However, we all learned how to handle a woman to get the information we need, among other needs fulfilled." AKA, they sleep with them and hope the sex is good enough to get them to forget who they are talking to. I roll my eyes.

"Would you rather be brought to a warehouse with all my toys or would you prefer a bed? I could spread you out on the table or take you to the shower if the other two aren't suitable."

I'd prefer the warehouse, but I don't say that out loud. I try to hide my blush when I realize what he'd be doing in those other places. "What would I prefer? This line of questioning to be over." I move in closer to him and place my hand over his heart to feel his pulse quicken. "If my memory is accurate, you wouldn't get anything out of me with the other methods. Who came first?"

I see his eyes flash. I know there is a lot of sexual tension between us.

We both want each other. I'm the one holding back. I close my eyes as he picks me up and throws me over his shoulder. I figure we are going to his bedroom, but I hear the ding of the elevator.

In no time, I'm being placed into the back seat of a black SUV that's out front of the building. Some random guy in a very nice suit is driving. "Where to boss?"

He keeps me nice and close to his side. "Warehouse Four." He says with authority. I mean the guy did call him 'boss'. He picks up his phone and stares at me. "Dad. Warehouse four is open tonight...perfect, it's now occupied...no, I'll get the information I need...sure, you can stop by...bring Matteo...I think he'll be helpful...see you soon."

The rest of the drive is quiet. However, I recognize this place. This is where he took me and watched me torture the two men for information after I called them to the other warehouse. "Is this your warehouse?" He nods. "I mean your's, not your family's."

He nods again. "They are one and the same. But this is where my people bring my charges. We each have our favorite one. This one happens to hold all my toys." He freezes when I go to open the door. "No. You do not exit a vehicle. Someone will open your door for you."

The driver opens my door and assists me out, which is weird. He also probably doesn't realize what I'm capable of. "You can go home. The others will be here soon so they can drop us off." Tony says as he comes to the other side of the car.

We walk inside as the car we arrived in leaves. His father and brother are already inside. "What are they doing here?"

I get a wicked grin as he takes my hand and leads me towards the chair in the middle of the floor. He sits me into the chair and steps back directly in front of me as he's flanked by his family. "Since you refuse to answer my questions, I figured you might open up to us."

I thought he was intelligent and now he lost all credit. I sigh because I'm most likely not going to be able to convince the three of them of the lies I could with only one of them.

"Since I don't think you'll answer my questions and you would probably prefer to be tortured instead of answering these questions. I had them bring someone in who will be tortured until you answer the questions."

My face gives me away right away. I can't let someone be tortured on my behalf. "What did he do?"

"Does it matter?" I nod because if he's a terrible person, no problem. If he's a good person, problem. "He has done nothing wrong." He smirks, but now I'm worried. I'm going to have an audience for all these questions and what he wants to know.

Chapter 10

Tony

I knew this was a risk, but I figured it would bring her fire out. When I texted my brother and asked him to pick up a guy, he picked someone we'd have to torture regardless. I just knew that I had to keep that information from her.

She's worrying her lip so I know she's actually considering telling us the truth. With an audience, which I know she'll hate, but I couldn't bluff alone. "How did he get here?" She asks the room. When my father goes to answer she just looks at the guy hung up. "You. How'd you get here." She demands. This isn't the same person that I watched torture not that long ago.

"I was driven." First rule: never lie when being questioned.

"Did you know where you were going when you were picked up?" She's figured this out that quickly?

"Yes. I was told I had to answer for my crimes." Maybe that was a terrible rule to give the men.

She looks at him then turns to look at us. Now she has the smirk. "Go ahead and torture him since you aren't letting him leave here alive. My failure to answer questions will not cause him to suffer since you were already planning it." She sits down in the chair.

I'm at a loss. My plan was to pull on her humanity. I didn't think she'd figure it out. "What are your feelings on death with dignity?" My father asks.

"You torture and kill, so what does it matter?" She responds.

Now, he's smirking as she works through his implication. "I don't care. I've done a lot in my lifetime, but you, well, I'm sure you have some limits. Yes, he was going to be killed regardless. However, I can make it quick or I can drag it out all night. The choice is yours. Answer these questions and he doesn't suffer. You don't get another…" I stop him before he finishes, where he is going will not help.

"Your choice." I say and shake my head at my father. He knows this is my show, I just need their support.

I've never had a sister or dealt with many females for questioning, but she groans as she sits in the most uncomfortable chair we have. "Fine. Ask."

"What are you planning?" That turns heads. She thought I was going to ask why she's going to hell.

Sighing, she settles. "Have someone kill me so they get the money for the hit. I would just need to know who put the hit on me first." I look at her instead of asking. "There's no point. I stayed for Alex. Yes, I was the youngest, but I've been his protector since our parents died. He couldn't handle violence even if he said he could. So, I learned who killed them and dealt with them. I used them as practice. I kept us alive and fed.

"He worked, like me, but he was always on the right side of the law. I took questionable clients and handled issues. Then, he went and fell in love. I told him how to stay out of harm's way, how to know if someone was following him, and how to make a quick, legal getaway. He'd tell me if anyone messed with him and I dealt with them." She stops.

I need to know why she's going to hell, but I can't ask in front of my father. He'll have her thinking she's a saint. I happen to love that she's not. Wait, love? I can't love her. "Why are you so ready to die?" This comes from Matteo.

"Because they are all gone and I should've gone first. They've done nothing wrong their entire lives yet I'm the one who has to live." She looks at him with tears in her eyes. She hates this. I hate that I put her in this situation, but until everything is cleared up and I'm not worrying about her doing something reckless, I can't stop. I've never felt guilted about any of the things I've done. They were always for protecting others. This is to protect her, but it's taking everything in me to not pick her up and tuck her into a nice, safe spot.

"What you did was to protect your family. You haven't done anything wrong." Of course, my father with the logic.

"You don't know what I've done. What I will do."

"Tell me. You think you are worse than me?" My father never talks during these. He makes us do it. I look at my brother and really take him in. They are both wearing what I typically wear to a warehouse because I get my hands dirty. Never them. They have, but it doesn't bother me. I've been doing this so long, not much does. But they stepped up for this one. Is it because of who she is? Our should-have-been in-law? Or is it something else? My brother looks at me; the answer in his face. It's something else; they figured it out already.

I try to keep calm, but all of a sudden, I can't breathe. The air isn't coming in, but it's going out. How can that happen? I don't see anything except the darkness that takes me.

***

I wake up back in my bedroom. The doctor is sitting next to me. When he sees me awake, he comes closer. "What was going through your head before you dropped?" There is never any judgment with him. But for the first time, I see worry. I tell him. All of it. As I get the words out, the panic comes back.

"Breathe. Slowly." He takes a deep breath himself. "How about I get you the answers?" He asks, but he's already sticking his head outside the door. I'm given no warning when she throws herself on top of me. Daniella is inspecting all of me.

"I'm fine. No need to worry." I say since she looks like she's been crying and about to start again. I kiss her forehead.

"I hate liars too you know." It's muffled, since she has her face buried in my chest.

"Tell him before this happens again." My eyebrows shoot up. My father is giving her orders and outing me all in the same sentence. He slams the door shut. I pull up the surveillance feed onto my tv as she settles next to me. I guess they are waiting for us to talk.

"I'm the reason my parents are dead. Their killer was looking for me and they wouldn't hand me over. I was young, but I was able to figure out who killed them and brought them to justice. I used him to learn how to get what I needed. Torture techniques, mainly. Once you kill someone, they tend to stay dead. I learned how to shoot and throw knives. Everything and anything. I taught myself. Alex was too kind. He looked to find the good in people and he understood violence, but felt other methods were better. I am the opposite."

She leans her head onto my chest, almost as if she can't look at me. "I tricked our brothers into meeting. I figured Matteo would be able to keep him safe. I hoped they would fall in love and live the lives they wanted. By setting them up, I put him in direct danger without knowing how to protect himself. So, yeah, I'm going to hell when the three of them are having a great reunion with everyone else in heaven."

I've remained quiet, but I know she's done talking. I tilt her chin so I can see her face. At least I'm fully functioning and not shot or something. "You did not cause their deaths. You did nothing to cause you to go to hell. You did everything to keep them safe. By handing yourself over to whoever wants you dead, that's not the answer. I need to know that you will at least work with me so you can stay alive. If you stay alive long enough, I'm sure we can make sure you go up instead of down." I swear, I will do anything and everything to stop from seeing her tears ever again.

"I can work with that." She whispers and I feel it. The weight lifts from my chest. I look down, but she's still nestled into my chest. So, what was that weight?

"Let's go make them all leave." I grab her hand and we walk into the living room where the three of them wait for me. I need to talk to the three of them separately, but I can't let Daniella hear.

As soon as my dad sees me, he nods and leaves. That's normal. I look at Matteo, which is all I need to do. "Daniella, can you show me something in the gym? I can't figure it out and Tony won't tell me."

When they are out of earshot, I turn to the doctor. "Feeling better?" He's assessing me like he does all of us.

"I think so. What happened to me?"

He gives me a smile, which is odd, since he never smiles. "You had a panic attack and passed out."

I blink. "That's never happened to me before. The passing out part. I wasn't in any danger. Why would it happen now? Do I need to worry about something?" I feel my heart start to race again, but I do the breathing thing he taught me.

"Whatever line of questioning you were doing with her, it led you to have anxiety about something. That is why I made you talk to her before you got out of bed. I'm guessing the weight on your chest is gone?"

"How did you know about the weight?" Did I wake up, tell him, and pass out again? That seems unlikely.

"It's a common thing with anxiety. The person feels like an elephant is sitting on them. I have a feeling this is completely related to that girl because typically you are terrifyingly steady." Doc shrugs like he is reading from a medical book and not discussing my personal life. The only thing he cares about with that is if we are being safe.

He takes my non-answer as a good way to leave. We keep him constantly busy with everything you can think of.

I go to the gym to talk to Matteo. When I reach the door, he is being shown some weird device that Daniella is walking him through. I'm fairly certain neither of them knows what to do since he's doing it wrong.

"Dani, do you mind giving us a minute?" I look back and forth between the two and keep the door open for her. When she is down the hallway, I lock the door behind me. I hate having my back to doors, but Matteo will watch it. Not that anyone is stupid enough to come here. Today has been too much. I just need to know one thing from him, but I don't know how to ask.

"It feels like taking a deep breath when you're drowning. The calmness of gliding down a mountain on a snowboard when nobody is around with fresh snow. The first person you think of when you want to share good news, and the first person you want to be next to you when you get bad news. The person you want to take grocery shopping with because they can make the most mundane things better." He walks towards the door, but stops when he reaches me. "She is your person and it's ok that you feel it this quickly." He pats my shoulder as he leaves.

***

After all the cards are on the table, we fall into a rhythm. We have breakfast together before going into the office. I typically drive us, but my dad has some soldiers following us. On nights I have work, she comes but doesn't participate. She's not afraid of what she sees me do. At least she hasn't said it bothers her. But at the end of the day, we sleep in the same bed. Nothing more than kissing has occurred, which is starting to get to me. It has never taken me this long to get a woman naked in my bed. But she's different.

I roll over and see she's still asleep. She's typically up before me and her eyes on me is what wakes me up. I know exactly how I want to wake her, my mouth between her legs, but she needs to make the first move. I've been getting the best sleep of my life since she started sharing my bed, though.

I sneak out to grab us coffee. I've learned a few things since she's been staying here. Her favorite foods, how she takes her coffee, and how to get her temper to show. I bring the mugs back to the bedroom and put hers on the side table. We even have our own sides of the bed.

I get my first look at her face this morning and freeze. She looks like she's in pain. I go to wake her because this isn't good. Right? Nobody should be in pain when they sleep. "Mostriciattola. Wake up. I got you coffee." She's usually hangry in the morning and refuses to talk before she has coffee and breakfast is started. I stroke my fingers across her check hoping to stir her awake.

Before I can take my next breath, my coffee is thrown across the room and I'm being flipped onto my back on my side of the bed with Dani on top of me. Yeah, that's a knife at my throat. I'm going to need to reevaluate how hot that was. I'm definitely twice as big as her, but that didn't matter.

11

Daniella

I don't know how we got into this position, but I have Tony on his back with my knife against his throat. I let the sleep leave my body before I move. Once I am awake and processed everything, I take in the man under me. I can't tell who is more shocked.

"Sorry about that." I sit back on my knees, which wasn't the best decision considering it lines up my softness with his hardness. "Sorry." I hurry off the bed. I look away from him and see the coffee that must have gone flying.

I break into cleaning mode. I run to the kitchen, grab all the cleaning supplies available and towels, before running back to the bedroom. I start cleaning. Once I get through the surface layer, I feel Tony staring at me for the second time. "Why are you staring at me?"

"I can't figure you out. One second you look like you're stuck in a nightmare and the next you go full lethal mode. Then, as soon as I have something figured out about you, you do the complete opposite. Also, I have a cleaning person that will deal with this." He still hasn't moved from the bed.

I shake my head. First, I'm not going to explain the nightmare, he's gotten too many of my secrets. Although, I am sleeping better than I ever have, which is either due to his presence or him getting me to open up and being lighter. "A stain like this needs immediate treatment. If it sits, it will get worse." I go back to scrubbing the stains. I can't deal with his look. I feel like he's staring into my soul and will unravel me completely.

"Stop." His hand stops mine. With just one touch, I feel the tears rush to find a way out, but I can't lose it again. After waking from that dream, I can't sit still or it will rush back. He has too many burdens already, I can't add this on top. He pushes my chin up so we are eye level. "Talk to me. What's going through that pretty head of yours?"

I don't want to lie anymore, but how do I explain? The tears start, but he wipes them away. I know he wants to pull me close, but I need to be able to think clearly, which doesn't happen when he's too close. "I need space." I whisper and go back to my bedroom to shower and change. This is our routine.

I'm about to step into the shower when my door opens. Well, that's one way to be caught naked. I go to try to grab something but as soon as I have the towel in my hand to wrap around me, it's ripped out of my hand. "No. You do not get space. I've given you space this entire week to let me in, but you haven't. So, no space. I need you. For some reason, I need you when I've never needed anything before in my life."

Finally. He herds me against the wall and picks me up. My legs instinctually go around his waist to pull him closer. I've been waiting for him to take control, but he has been a saint. Never making the first move after I've pushed him away. Only kissing my forehead. Since he said it was his choice to risk his heart, I've been wanting him to show me they were more than just words.

I gasp as he increases the urgency of the kiss and he takes the opening. He doesn't leave any part of my mouth unexplored. As soon as he breaks the kiss, I see the questions in his eyes. But I have one of my own. "What took you so long?"

"You to give me permission. I told you I was ready to risk my heart. I was waiting on you." He nips at my bottom lip as he kisses me again. This time with less aggression, but more passion. "I won't wait as long next time. Go ahead and get ready. I'll meet you in the kitchen."

I take the longest shower possible. As much as I didn't want that kiss to end, I have a feeling we will be exploring each other tonight. Hopefully, he doesn't get called to a warehouse. I get dressed in the most conservative outfit possible. I need to get something done in the office today. I think I've figured out another one of Hal's schemes. If I am redoing their accounting practices, I need to know everything he has screwed up.

I usually make us breakfast, but maybe we will just grab something on the way in. They do have a bunch of options in the office if we don't get anything. I smell something burning and rush into the kitchen with one shoe on. Tony is standing in front of the stove and toaster, but he's looking up at the smoke detector that is beeping.

I jump onto the counter and deal with the detector. Then, I turn the stove off and take out whatever he put in the toaster. "Let's just get breakfast in the office." I toss him the keys after I put my other shoe on. I grab my bag after calling the elevator. When the elevator arrives, he still isn't here. "Tony, let's go!" He looks ashen as he enters the elevator.

***

There were no words spoken in the car or on the way up to the office. He walked right to his office and closed the door. I hoped we would have some lighthearted banter or some touching. Ever since I found him in the kitchen, it's like he's been possessed.

I drop my bag and grab some breakfast before locking myself into my office. Halfway through the day, a knock interrupts my thoughts and search. In walks Matteo, he looks off. I'm glad the three of them don't wait for an invitation. It makes me feel like they are comfortable with me and I don't need to fear them. "What happened this morning?"

I feel my face flush, but he can't be referencing that. Instead of letting him in on something that we aren't even sure about. "He was making breakfast and burned something. The smoke detector went off and it was almost like he was in a trance."

"Could you smell the burnt items?" This is weird. Why would something burning be a problem?

"Yes. I dealt with it, though. I turned the smoke detector off, got rid of the burnt items. He hasn't spoken since I found him staring at the smoke detector." I answer him, but as he turns to leave, I'm confused. "What's going on?"

He keeps walking to Tony's office. Well, I'm following. He can't assume that I would not be interested in knowing what actually is going on. It was burnt toast, which I happen to love. When we get to his office, Matteo looks me over. "You might want to let me handle this."

"I'm not going anywhere." I stand my ground. I have a feeling he knows what I'm not saying.

He sighs as he knocks on the door where we are given a grunt. I guess he still isn't talking? I look over his shoulder to get a view of Tony's office, but all I see is an empty decanter on his desk with one glass that is full. "Do you have scotch?" If I didn't see the empty decanter, I would now know he is drunk and it isn't even lunch time. He hasn't eaten today, so all the liquor went right to his head.

"Alright, let's get you home. I'm guessing you drove and will not allow Dani to drive you home. So, I'll have one of the guys drive you back. Dani, are you able to work from his place today since I don't want Tony left alone?"

"Daniella. She's so pretty. Did you hear that I got to kiss her this morning? I'm ready for tonight where I'm going to make her mine. Do you think she'll let me in? I know I'm a mess, but I want to keep her. Do you think I should propose?" Oh boy, he's really drunk and he doesn't realize I'm here.

Matteo just looks over at me. "I think you should hold off on proposing. Maybe talk it over first?"

Tony sighs and grabs the glass. He downs the rest of the contents. "She's turned me into a cuddler. I was never a cuddler, but she just puts every piece back together."

"Ok. Well, we will revisit all of this tomorrow when you aren't drunk including why you felt the need to drink so much to get drunk. I'll walk you two down."

"Who else is coming?" Just then Matteo steps aside to show Tony that I've been standing here. "How much of what I just said did she hear?" I can tell he's trying to whisper, but it's loud enough for everyone.

74

"The entire thing. I'm going to grab my bag and laptop. I'll meet you two at the elevators." I turn to leave because I need some space now that I know he wants to propose. I was only agreeing to sex this morning. Not a relationship. The drive to the apartment is awkward. Neither of us know what to say. Tony is still unaware of me being here.

I hear Matteo tell the driver to stay downstairs as he escorts us upstairs. After getting Tony settled, he pulls me into the kitchen. "One of my guys is going to stay downstairs if you need anything. Don't let anyone in. My dad and I both have access cards to get in, so we don't knock." With that, he turns and leaves us alone.

***

Tony slept the entire afternoon in his bed alone. I managed to get him to eat something, drink an entire bottle of water, and take something. He then proceeded to tell me how I'm the best teddy bear. I thought he fell back asleep when I heard him start talking.

He understood why I blame myself for my family's deaths because he is the reason his mother left. Apparently, he burnt toast and his mother screamed at him, left and never came back. So now, even after all this time has passed, when he smells burnt toast, he freezes. That seemed a tad extreme. I thought I'd have to wait for answers, but he kept talking. He told me how his father found out his mother cheated on him and she was never spoken about again. He told me about his induction into the family and what he had to do. How he became the best interrogator in the family. Why he felt he would never have what our brothers' had.

But my favorite part was about his relationship with Matteo. How they were always close, but got even closer after their mom left. It reminded me of my relationship with Alex.

After I left him in his bed, I got myself ready and as soon as I was getting into the bed, my door flies open. Tony stares at me. His steps are steadier, but his eyes give him away. "I'm not sleeping without you ever again." Then, he crawled into my bed and pulled me to him.

That was a few hours ago. I managed to get out of his death grip since I was starting to bruise. The first time I got away, he pulled me back. The second time, I handcuffed him to the bed. I'm not proud, but I need some sleep as well.

When I finally start to drift off, I hear the elevator open. "Find him. Now." Great, whisper-yelling. My room doesn't have access to the security feed, so I can't watch but they aren't quiet. I pick up my phone and dial Mr. Segreto. Hopefully, he's still awake. It's about to go to voicemail and I'm about to try Matteo, when he answers. "Daniella. What is it?"

"Hurry." It's all I can say. I put the phone on the dresser by the door as I get into position. One guy barges into the room and I hit him over the head with the butt of Tony's gun. I might have brought it in from his room. The next one points a gun in my face, so I use my stun gun on him. I hear footsteps rushing away from this room. I've never been happier the door is an elevator.

As I turn the corner, I notice he doesn't have a gun pointed at me, which is odd. "This doesn't concern you, whore." Well, that's one way to make a first impression. He doesn't know I've been called everything in the book.

I let a smile cross my face as I pick up the extremely heavy vase from the table, which I throw at his head. He doesn't duck in time, but now there is blood on the floor. I found rope the other day in the front closet when I was snooping, so I drag the man to the kitchen and tie him up.

The two guys in the bedroom doorway are still out, so I do the same to them. After making sure Tony is still asleep, I grab my phone and close the door after grabbing some pants. No reason for Matteo and their dad to see me without pants on. I then pull up a chair and wait for them to arrive.

When I hear the elevator open, I grab the gun, but quickly lower it. Thankfully, it's his family. His dad looks like he is ready to torture everyone before killing them and wants to take all night. But Matteo, he looks ready to kill everyone so he can go back to bed. Don't get me wrong, I'm glad they came, but I think I should be the one to kill them. Just not here. I don't want to deal with the mess or having a clean-up crew arrive and drag out the night any more than it already has been.

I don't know how I missed the bellhop tied up between the two of them. "What is he doing here?"

Mr. Segreto drags the bellhop over to the other three I have tied up already. "First, where is my son? Are you ok?" He then spins me around while assessing me. "How did you get those three tied up?"

"He's still sleeping. He won't be joining us since he's handcuffed to the bed. I'm fine, not even a scratch on me." Surprising even myself, I give him a hug. "Thanks for coming." I've never called someone asking for help and they actually show up. I stopped asking after everyone I thought would help didn't show up.

"Why's he handcuffed?" Of course, Matteo would ask.

"He kept trying to use me as a teddy bear. He was squeezing too much, so I handcuffed him." This time at least. I'm going to need to show Tony where the latches are so he can get himself out of a bind.

Chapter 12

Tony

All the noise wakes me. I go to put the pillow over my head, but I can't move my arms. I went to sleep in my bedroom, but that's not where I am. I look around and realize I'm in Dani's room. I start trying to figure out how to get out of the fuzzy handcuffs, but I've never been in handcuffs before.

I pull at my hands and the headboard breaks. I remain handcuffed and follow the sound of calm voices. Entering the living room, there are four men tied up, one being my bellhop. The other three were made men. What drew my attention was Dani *hugging* my dad. I can't remember the last time he hugged anyone, which explains why he looks so uncomfortable.

I wasn't expecting a full family reunion at some weird hour. I don't even know what time it is. I also don't want to face my family, including my dad, while in handcuffs. Luckily, Daniella comes over to me and hands me a water after uncuffing my hands. I look at her face and realize it's bright red. Only then do I realize I'm naked.

After running back to my room and grabbing a pair of pants since I have no intention of torturing someone naked. They don't get a free show. I do wonder how many questions I'm going to have to field when this is over about why I was naked and handcuffed in her bed.

78

"Alright. Someone fill me in. Why are there four men tied up in my living room?" I look around the room. I recognize two of the three since he's one of ours. "What the hell?" I'm not waiting for answers. This will sober me up quicker anyway.

I go to start hitting our made man, but my arm is stopped. Daniella has my arm and is shaking her head at me. It's not her choice if I torture them here, but my dad is looking at me like I've lost it.

"We are discussing if we should move them to a warehouse for easy clean up." She whispers to me like I'm not the one who typically handles these situations.

"We will deal with them how I see fit." I don't mean to be so forceful, but to her credit, she just laughs. Not a chuckle, a full belly laugh with a snort.

I look to my dad since he's the boss. "She's the one who tied them up and kept you safe. She also called me. You can try to tell her what to do, but it's her show. I'm just here to make sure she remains safe and to hear the answers. He's here," nodding to Matteo, "since I thought we'd need extra hands."

She did this? Incapacitated and tied up three made men? I know we never harm females, but we can control them without hurting them. She's tiny and outnumbered. And she's still laughing. I muster up all the calmness I can. "Why are you against dealing with this situation here?"

That snaps her out of the laughter. Her eyes still shine with glee, like she's lighting up from the inside. She knows she won. "Two reasons. One, I don't want more people in here after we deal with them. I know it can take a while to clean up after what will be occurring and I would like to get some sleep. I know I won't sleep if there are a bunch of men right outside the bedroom. Two, if someone hears what is occurring, they might call the police. Yes, it would be rare, but I don't want them walking in on this. Even though they should know better, someone might be easily pursued to flip and turn state's witness. So, I'd rather not kill a cop."

Well, shit. Those are extremely good and valid reasons. I guess were going to the warehouse. "I'll call ahead. Can you get them into cars or should I wake some of my guys up?" I specifically have a number of my men living in this building for this reason.

"Call three up. I don't feel like doing all the heavy lifting." Matty answers. I go to my room and get dressed and make arrangements. By the time I'm ready to go, two of the men are gone and one of my men stands with my dad and brother while openly assessing Dani.

She's still in her pajamas, which leave little to the imagination. "Dani. A word." She turns and nods to my dad before following me into her bedroom. She looks exhausted. I should make her stay behind, but I like keeping my balls attached. She goes to her clothes and throws stuff on the bed. With the broken headboard. Now, I'm checking her out and this is not the time.

"Talk. I'll change while I listen." You can hear sleep trying to pull her under. The adrenaline must finally be wearing off.

"Why didn't you wake me?" I have a lot of other things, but I'm hurt she went to my dad first. He should have been the second one she went to. I watch her pull her tank top off and see a gun in her waistband. "Why do you have one of my guns?" That's definitely not important, but that's mine. Does she know how to use it? I try not to focus on her perky breasts since I shouldn't have a hard on while torturing. That's just weird, but it's hard not to notice.

"I tried, but you swatted me. Or tried to, at least. I knew you were still drunk and I didn't want you as a liability. This way I was fully focused on the men. When you joined me in bed after we talked, I went back and put the one on your nightstand next to you. I figured you were used to sleeping with one close and I didn't want you to be unprepared. I grabbed it when I heard people enter." She hands the gun to me before changing her pants.

I hate how logical she sounds. How is she able to think logically after what happened? "What happened?" That should have been my first question. As I listen to her tell me, in detail, everything that happened, I'm more than ready to hurt them. I don't care if they are after me. I get it, but she's off limits.

"Are you ready to go? I'd like to have this completed within an hour so I can sleep at least a little." She walks to the door, but doesn't open it until I nod. We have a lot to talk about tomorrow, or maybe it's later today. After we sleep, we'll talk.

We go back into the living room and my dad is the only one left. "How you holding up?" He looks at Daniella, who shrugs. Well, I guess he has a new favorite child. He always wanted a girl. With how amazing she is, I don't blame him, I want her too. "I'll drive. The boys went ahead to get everything prepared for you." Again, it's like I don't even exist.

***

The car ride was painful. Not because of the hangover I'm sure to have, but my dad put Dani in the passenger seat and pushed me into the back. Then, the two of them ignored me the entire time. They talked about everything and anything. I tried to cut in, but my dad glared at me through the rearview mirror.

When we arrive, Dani waits until one of us opens her door, which was me. Thankfully, she remembered that rule. I take her hand in mine as we walk into the warehouse. Three men are suspended from the ceiling. "Where's the fourth?" I hope I wasn't seeing double and saw more people.

"I killed him. He failed in his capacity by giving someone access to your home." Matteo shrugs. Well then. I don't blame him, but it would have been nice to watch. Or do.

"These are all sanctioned, so don't worry." Dad says this to us. They broke in, so I'd say very sanctioned.

"Two answers. That's all I want. Alright?" Dani says to the three of them. They all turn their eyes to her. "First, who were you trying to kill?" I guess honey does better than vinegar, because they all look at me. Three made men, and they just broke that easily.

"Excellent. Second, why?" When nobody answers, she continues. "I know. This is a harder one. You have to use your brain and really put the words together." She moves over to the table of tools. My tools, but I'll share this time. She picks them up, one at a time like she is seeing which one talks to her, but she continues talking. "Look, tonight is going to end with you three dead. That's a given. You have no say in that. However, you can be tortured first or you can skip that part and get a bullet in the head. Quick and easy, no pain. That part, that's up to you."

She turns and faces them with tools I've never used together. My eyes light up like Christmas morning. I'm finally going to learn something! "I'll tell you what. I'll explain, with detail, how I'd torture you. Then, I'll let you decide the route we take to the bullet. Fair?"

Shockingly, they don't answer. Not shockingly, they are now pale. I know this is her show, but I can't sit still anymore. "Mostriciattola." That gets everyone's attention. "I've never used those two together. What are you thinking?" I go stand behind her, looking over her shoulder so I can see her motions and their reactions.

She looks ready to be devoured. She likes that I don't mind, hell, I love her willingness to get her hands dirty. "Thanks for asking. First, I'd use this one." She waves her right hand. "I'd make sure to get a good grip on one of their balls. Then I'd use this one. Well, it's self-explanatory from that point. Don't you think?" Damn. That's just vicious.

She turns to face me and lifts up to her toes before whispering 'later' into my ear and biting my earlobe. "So, now that you know what the lady wants to do, who'd like to go first?"

"You cutoff the drug supply into the southside. We were benefiting from those sales." The one on the end stutters.

"Cutting off the drug supply? That was not my decision to make. Why would I be the one you attack?" I shouldn't be asking. That's stupid enough. Our family doesn't even deal with drugs. Our contribution to the five families is money laundering. Each family has a specific contribution that helps everyone and it ranges from drugs to port control.

They hesitate. I hold my hands for the tools and she gives them over. "Our capo said you were the one making these decisions. You are trying to take over the families and make yours the leader. He confirmed it." He gives a pointed look to our man.

He confirmed a lie? Why? I shoot the other two. I grab Daniella's hand and bring her to my dad. "I'm going to be busy for a while. Do you think you can take her to your house so she can get a good night's sleep?"

I think I broke my dad. He looks like I'm not speaking English. Maybe I slipped into Italian? I do that when I'm super drunk or excited. It's hard to not revert back to your first language. "I'm not going anywhere. He betrayed this family and I will not stand for that." He looks at Matty.

"I'll take her to the house. I'm ready to go back to sleep. Call if you need me. Can you call ahead?" He looks worse than she does. I wonder if he hasn't slept since before Alex died too. Maybe they were staying at each other's place and couldn't sleep without the other. That's how I am and I haven't even fucked her yet.

My dad and I watch the two of them leave the warehouse. Now, I get to have fun.

***

Usually, I like to draw out the torture, but I have a beautiful woman to get home to. Hopefully, she'll be ready for whatever promises she was going to make. I feel like we are just waiting to combust. Maybe we both feel that this is it. We will never have anything better after having each other. My dad and I got all the answers we needed before my dad put a bullet in his head. We called in a clean-up crew and left. Nothing has been said since we got in the car.

When we pull onto his street, he starts talking. "Do you love her?" I know it's a question, but I don't know how to answer. Love? I never imagined finding someone to love.

"I'm not sure. Ever since I met her, I can't get her out of my head. She's invaded every part of me and I think I like it? No other woman has ever made me feel like I can be my full true self. But Daniella. She sees all of me, every flaw and dark corner, she's not my shining light, but she gets me out of the darkness."

He nods. No words of wisdom. "Why haven't you told her that?" Again, a simple question with no simple answer.

"She doesn't want me to become Matteo. She thinks her time is limited with the hit. She doesn't think she is good enough to be given love."

"Better to be loved and lost than never loved at all. Some famous person said that. It's true. Love her like every second could be your last and maybe, she'll realize her feelings for you. Trust me, even a week full of love is better than never risking your heart." I'm staring at him. What did he do to my father?

"I thought you never loved mom?" This is the weirdest conversation I've ever had with my dad. Harming others, fine; running businesses, all the time; family organization, of course; but love, never; mom, even before she was caught, never.

He chuckles. "Her. No, I never loved her. Right before I was told I was marrying her, I met Alice. I fell for her. Hard and fast. No time to even realize I had before it was too late. I planned to marry her. Then, my father decided I would marry your mother. He had Alice killed. Made me dig her grave and everything. So, I know that it is better to risk your heart even if you only have a short time together." He parks the car in front of his entrance. I'm stunned. Why would his father do that? "Have no fear, I won't harm her. You boys get to choose who to marry."

I watch him enter the house. Two of his men are stationed outside. We already passed the guards at the gate. Maybe I should get Dani a home? That's ridiculous. I don't even know if she wants to be with me. I go into the house. Stop for waters in the kitchen before going to my room. Hopefully, Matteo put her there and not in one of the many other rooms.

Chapter 13

Daniella

Strong, warm arms running down my spine wake me. I heard Tony come home and climb into bed, but I don't know when that was. At least he wasn't squishing me like last time. Sighing, I turn to face him. He's lying on his side with his full chest on display.

"Good morning." He says while kissing my hair. "I couldn't wait any longer. Are you still tired?" He keeps rubbing my back while pulling me closer.

I nod into his chest. I could use another few hours, but the tension between us is too much. I want to go back to sleep but after I explore. "I'm sorry about yesterday. I shouldn't have gotten so drunk and been unable to protect you. I also shouldn't have questioned why you called my dad when people came in." He sighs.

I can tell he's about to continue, but he doesn't know that I know. "What do you remember about yesterday? Specifically, between getting back from the office and when you saw your family in the living room." I pause when I see the wheels start turning.

"Nothing. I don't even remember coming into your room." He answers quietly.

I give him a soft smile so he doesn't panic. "You woke up, had something small to eat, drank water, and took some medicine. After I tucked you back in, you got up and climbed into my bed, tried to use me as a personal teddy bear, which is why you were handcuffed. However, before you feel back asleep, you told me why you drank yourself stupid. I have no issue with how you are coping. I just need two things from you: talk to me, don't leave me in the dark, ever and I don't need you to protect me, I want us to protect each other. I did what I had to when I called your dad."

As the words come out, the hands on my back stop. When I finish, he sits up and moves away from me. "What did I say?" I give him the full rundown and watch his face turn red. "I shouldn't have forced all that on you." I watch him get up and go into the bathroom after slamming the door.

I follow him in. I know he wants to be alone, but he isn't anymore. I turn the shower on and start undressing. He only has pants on, so once I finish, I undress him. I pull him into the shower and once we are both clean, I go to turn off the water, but he stops my hand. He has to take the lead. I don't want to push him too far if he isn't ready. He had a rough twenty-four hours.

I see the question in his eyes. He wants this. Might even need this. I nod before taking his mouth with mine. I let myself enjoy the feel of his mouth and the tentativeness of him. I hear him growl and it turns needy. He can't get enough of me. I can't keep up with him. He pulls me tight against him and I have no idea how we are going to stay on our feet.

He forces me back toward the wall while running his hands up and down my arms. We might be in the steam filled shower with the hot water running, but his touch is raising goosebumps with anticipation. When my back hits the wall, his hands slide behind me to lift me up. This will not be slow and explorative. This is going to hard and rough. I'll get what I want later.

As soon as he's positioned, he slowly lowers me onto his hard length. I feel him slowly push into my entrance. As much as he'd like to thrust into me, I can tell he doesn't want to cause any pain, but I need him in me. I pull my mouth away from his. He freezes. "Don't be gentle." I say before biting on his bottom lip and pulling his mouth back to mine.

I don't know if it was the words or the action, but he thrusts into the hilt before pausing again. This time, I let him, I don't know how he fit all the way, but the sensations are almost too much. I start moving to let him know I'm ready. Honestly, I need him to move.

Without another word, he picks up the pace and before I know it, I'm coming. I feel my muscles clench around him as I start coming. He follows without fail. He doesn't stop until we are both breathing heavy and fully sated. After pulling out, he settles me onto my feet. I have no clue how my legs are holding me, but they do.

He quickly washes our bodies like I did before. This time, he turns off the water and covers me with a towel before grabbing one for himself. I should get ready for the rest of the day. I should go into the office.

But, all my shoulds don't happen when Tony pulls me back to bed. I'm lying on my side, basically on top of him, while he's on his back. "I don't want to burden you with my life, especially the past. There's a lot I can't share with you for your safety. I should let you go, but I can't. I want to keep you. I've never wanted someone so much in my life. I should be happy you were smart enough to call my dad and handle the men, but I want you safe where no one can ever harm you."

I'm starting to think his squeezing of me is just his way to make sure I'm still there and to keep me close. "You aren't burdening me. You are setting yourself free by sharing your life with me. I want to know. I get there are certain things can't share, but I don't want you to hold back. I can handle it."

"I can't risk your life." I can tell he is terrified of losing me. It doesn't make sense with how little we've known each other. But, I know exactly how he feels.

I push up so I can look into his eyes. "You aren't risking my life. I'm deciding if I want to risk something. I'll always protect you even if you don't agree with how I do it. I'm not the type of person that would want to be hidden away and kept safe. That's not who you'd want. I'm happy you decided to risk your heart on me." After the words are out, I press a soft, short kiss to his lips before settling back down.

"My dad never loved my mom. His father killed the love of his life and told me I should try to keep you happy as long as possible." I feel the truth in his words and close my eyes. I've never liked talking feelings. With him, I don't want anything to remain unsaid even if I can't say the words I feel. It's too soon. I don't understand how I could feel this after only knowing him for such a short period.

I let myself nestle into him more, but once his words fully register, I shoot up. "Is your dad planning to kill me so he can marry you off?"

He chuckles and pulls me back down. "No. He explicitly said who my brother and I choose to marry and love is up to us. Also, I can't remember the last time my father gave me a hug and I watched him ignore me on the way over to the warehouse. He is also impressed how you managed to tie up three men, but responsible enough to call him."

I smile into his chest and let the sleep take over.

***

This time when I wake up, the man beside me is still sleeping with his arms under his pillow. I slip out of the covers and go straight to the bathroom. After getting ready for the day, I go in search of coffee. Unfortunately, I am wearing Tony's pants and t-shirt since I didn't pack a bag of clothes when we left for the warehouse.

The kitchen was easier to find than expected. The coffee is still hot, so I pour myself a mug before raiding the fridge. Is it weird that I'm raiding my future father-in-law's fridge without supervision? Wait. Future father-in-law? We had sex once and now I'm thinking about marriage? Don't get me wrong, it was great, but I never imagined getting married. Even when I was young and girls were discussing the perfect wedding, I didn't understand why someone would do that. It's just a day, but now, marriage? Can you even marry into the mafia?

Well, at least my brain is still functioning, but I need coffee and food and work before I go down a slippery slope. I turn and speak of the devil, he's watching me. "Can I make you something?" I can't trust what words will come out, so I nod. "Have a seat at the counter. How are you feeling? Did you sleep well?"

This is weird. One second, I'm thinking about having a father-in-law, the next, that same man, comes into the kitchen to feed me. I get it, not that weird since he owns the house, but still. "Fine, thanks. I just need to do something. I won't sleep tonight since I fell back asleep, so I'm thinking I'll go into the office. I don't want to disturb anyone or disrupt your sleep."

I guess he's cooking skills aren't that great since he's making me a bowl of cereal. Until he ruins it with milk. What happens if I refuse to eat something in his kitchen? I opened a few cabinets and there are weapons everywhere. Not to mention the block of knives right next to him. "You are not going into the office. If you want to work, I'll have someone bring over a computer and I'll set you up in an office." He passes the bowl across the island, but I just stare at it. Got it, nobody tells him what they are going to do.

I look from him to the bowl and back again. Hopefully, he realizes before he asks. "Right. Sorry, I completely forgot." I sigh. At least this way I'm not being rude. "Here you go." Handing me a spoon.

Nodding, I look at the bowl again. Nope, I can't do it. Placing the spoon down. "I can't eat this." I push the bowl back.

"Do you feel sick? You said you were fine."

Before he can finish calling whoever, I speak up. No need for more people to get involved. "It's the milk. I can't have dairy. I should have said something earlier, but I didn't see you take it out or pour."

He puts his phone down, grabs a new bowl, and just pours cereal in before passing it to me. "I will eat this bowl then if you don't mind me joining you." He sits on the stool next to me. I'm sure we look funny like this. I'm on the smaller side for females and he is definitely on the larger side, but that's not the reason. I'm wearing his son's clothes which don't fit at all and he's in a full suit, only missing a tie.

We eat in silence because I have no clue what to talk about. "Are you Catholic?" Whiplash would have hurt me less. I didn't hear him correctly, right?

"No, not Catholic. Why?" I have no clue what direction this conversation will go in.

"Can't get married in our church then. Non-traditional I guess." He's talking to himself, but I hear him. Why couldn't I have terrible hearing instead of eyesight? "Matty won't be getting married in the church either. I guess we could try new traditions." He keeps talking like I'm not here.

"Who's getting married?" From what I've figured out, Matteo is still mourning my brother, which is fine. I want him to move on, but you can't rush grief. Especially since he didn't know he was dead and hated him before I showed up.

"Nobody yet, I just like to have plans or ideas of what will happen. I had your brother's wedding planned after he asked permission." Great, they are all on board with Tony and I getting married. Did he insert a mind reading chip into me at some point? Also, when did he do it?

"Thanks for the food. I'll clean up. If it's not too much to ask, could you have my laptop from Tony's penthouse dropped off? Or I could go get it if we are staying here longer. I just need to do something and work is the best option since I'm not planning anyone's wedding." I take my bowl to the sink and clean it before putting it in the dishwasher.

I go to grab his, but he's holding it still. "You both will be staying here until I know those men weren't lying. I also want the names of whomever gave them that information. I'll have someone take you to get some clothes and the computer. I don't want you alone, though."

After he says all that, he slides the bowl over. Great. Living with Mr. Segreto now too. Does he know we had sex? Is it weird to have sex under your parent's roof? Maybe we should pause anything physical while we're here. Where is his bedroom? We were not quiet. Luckily, the shower and bathroom muted some of the noise? Tony needs to wake up. Now.

"Do you have a gun?" Wow, these questions are everywhere.

"Just my stun gun. I have a taser, but it's in my car that I haven't seen." Maybe I can get my car back. But if I can't be alone, I can't drive alone. I'll convince the follower to let me drive. How hard can that be?

He blinks. At least I know where Tony and Matteo get their poker faces from. "Do you know how to use a gun?" I nod. "Why don't you have one?"

"Easy. I don't need one. If I need to shoot someone, I use their gun. That way they can't trace the gun to anyone except the victim. Also, what would an accountant need a gun for?"

"Well, you work for shady people. You should be better armed. But that is a good reason to not have one. I'll get one of my men to drop an untraceable one off for you to have. Any preferences?" I know I shouldn't ask for anything crazy like purple. I think that would stand out too much. There is something. "What is it? Nothing is too much for this."

I bet a bazooka would be too much. I keep that inside though. Both of us don't need to be voicing our inner thoughts. "An ambidextrous grip, please. Maybe something small enough to fit in a purse?" I have no clue what that would be, but he nods and types it into his phone. I wonder who is going to pick it out?

Chapter 14

Tony

I wake to an empty bed. Her side is cold, so she's been gone a while. I immediately jump up. At least I'm not handcuffed again. Although, I would like those to be used in a different manner. I open the door at the same time she is trying to enter. Happily, she falls into my outstretch arms. Unluckily, she is wearing my clothes, which is making me harder than I've ever been.

"I was going to leave you a note. I'm running back to your place to get a few things. Your dad wants us to stay here until the threat is fully handled." She was going to leave without me? At least she was going to leave a note so I didn't panic, which I was already doing.

"Give me five minutes and I'll take you." I release her and head towards the bathroom.

"Sorry, your dad said you can't leave. I'm going with a few of his men and I'll be in and out in ten minutes tops. You have a closet full of clothes here, but is there anything special I should grab?" She is standing by the door. I want to pull her in and kiss her again, but if my dad is sending his men, he's waiting.

"No, I don't th…" I didn't use a condom this morning. I've never not used one. I know I'm clean and I bet she is too, but I'm not stupid. I would love to see her pregnant though. I bet she'd make perfect babies. Wait. Slow down brain, we can't start down that path. "Do you want kids?" Yup, brain isn't listening.

She goes through a ton of emotions while opening and closing her mouth. "What is with your family? I don't know if I want to get married, I don't know if I want kids. I'm not even sure I'll live through the week. Text me if you need anything." She turns to leave.

"Condoms." That stops her. "We didn't use one in the shower this morning, which is on me. But if you don't want kids, maybe you should grab the box from my nightstand." This shouldn't be a weird conversation after what happened earlier, but I can feel the tension. Not the fun kind.

"Anything else?" Her voice sounds small. I hope I didn't mess this up before we gave it a real shot. I quietly walk towards her and block her path from leaving. I kiss her. Softly. Nothing like earlier. No, this is the type of kiss we should have started with. I feel her melt into me and when I feel her wanting more, I pull back. "I'm on the pill, so don't worry."

That's all she says as she pushes me aside and leaves. I stand in my doorway watching her disappear. What am I supposed to say? Great, still want to be safe or why don't you stop and we can make babies? Yeah, the latter option is not a good idea. I need to figure out why we are being trapped here. Her, I love that idea. Me, not really an option.

***

I take another shower, get dressed, and go on a search of my father. I know this is something we need to discuss. This isn't an order he can give me anymore. When I was younger and not as involved, fair order. He wants Matteo to take over and me to step back from enforcer duties, we're going to talk.

He's in the first place I look. Of course, I stopped in the kitchen for coffee first. I can't deal with anyone except a certain firecracker without caffeine. I knock on his open door. One of the first things we learned growing up, an open door doesn't mean enter unless you want a bullet. My dad assesses me in the doorway before nodding to the chair in front of his desk. I will never sit in that position. At least that's the hope.

Only his most trusted men are allowed into the house, but none of them have free reign. However, with everything going on, I close the door before sitting. "Why did Dani inform me that I'm not allowed to leave?"

He knew this was coming, but I don't think she was supposed to say anything. "She asked to go to the office and I said no. We had a discussion and this is what we agreed to. She can leave with my protection until the threat against you is handled in its entirety."

"Why can she leave, but not me?" Honestly, I am more than capable of protecting myself. He made sure of it. He doesn't know what she can do outside of a warehouse.

"You sound like a five-year-old." He scolds. "Matteo is doing ground work to make sure the threat was eliminated last night. I am having discussions with the other families to make sure they haven't heard anything. It's not going to be a long-term stay."

There is only one thing that keeps coming to my thoughts and I know it'll piss him off. "Is she safe here? Does anyone even know she was at my place last night?"

"Of course, she is safe." He scoffs. "But I have someone dropping off a present for her later today. They will not enter the home, but I don't want him to see her. That will keep her safe. From what I hear, you haven't taken anyone to bed since she started her assignment. So, yes, people probably know."

He doesn't seem to want to budge on me leaving. "I can run the companies from here. I don't need to be in the office, but what about my nightly duties? I don't feel comfortable letting someone else handle that fully."

"There are two people fully capable of handling those duties. One being Matteo and the other being Daniella. If I need her, she said she can handle it if I let her know what we need from them." He says it so nonchalantly, but he's going to send her in my place?

"Why are you ok with her getting involved in the family business? Usually, any and all women are kept out of it. Why her?" I can't sit still anymore. He knows my feelings. Well, he's guessed at them and I haven't denied anything. Plus, he's more observant than anyone thinks.

He finishes his glass, which is uncommon. He drinks, but not this early usually. Something must be pissing him off. I have a feeling it's the fact someone is trying to kill me, not me specifically. "Because you would never want to be with someone without being able to share your life with them. She can handle this world. Plus, she was not deterred when she found out what you do for me." He gets up and hands me a drink after refilling his. "I also saw her abilities. It helps that she isn't reckless. She knows when to get backup, but she handled those three men without a scratch on her. She kept her head and didn't make a mess."

Damnit. I hate this. "Fine. But I want to leave soon. Even if it's just to go on a drive. I can't be stuck inside this entire time." I don't wait for a dismissal. He knows better than to keep me in more than a few days. I don't do well when I'm contained. I never have been.

Now, I need to figure out what do with the rest of my time before Dani gets back. If I'm going to be stuck here, I need my computer, so I text Dani. I go to the kitchen to find something to eat. One positive about staying here, we'll have complete meals prepared of us.

***

I'm swimming laps when I hear splashing. Looking up, a capo is standing by the edge in a suit with my dad not too far away. I swear none of the men know how to dress the part. Unless that part is funeral. I grab a towel and my water before joining them.

"We're going to a dinner meeting." Aka my dad is going to a meeting where the capo will stay outside by the car with the others. "Do not leave the property. I would like you inside before dusk." I feel like I'm a child again, but I didn't have restrictions then. There were a ton more men around when we were small. Apparently, we were a handful and dad didn't trust nannies after mom.

I look at the sky and see it is past the time I'm supposed to be inside. I follow them in but stop in the kitchen as they continue to the foyer. I grab two plates for dinner and go in search of a certain housemate who might be hungrier for something else.

I've been to our bedroom, every living room and dining room, the game room, gym, and two of the offices. I can't find her. I haven't had a chance to put a tracker on her phone, but that wouldn't be specific enough. They usually only say the address. I would call her, but her cell is in our bedroom.

She's hiding in the fifth office I checked. Headphones on. Tapping away at the keyboard like she is on a mission. I knock at the door, but it's no use. Since she won't look up and these plates are getting heavy, I slide the food right in front of her, which is also on her keyboard.

Instead of a smile, I get a look I haven't seen before. "What's wrong?"

An audible swallow is never good. "I got my work computer from your place. Yours is in our room, by the way. Your dad has me writing new procedures for all the accounting across all the companies, which is easier than doing separate ones for legit and non-legit. I've been reading the old ones to see what we can keep and there is nothing. It seems your father's boss wrote them and your dad just accepted them. I started looking into Hal and it seems he was the one assisting with writing them."

I sit in the chair. I was going to eat, but that's now forgotten. Which is sad since it was Bolognese. "So, Hal and my grandfather were working together to steal from the family business?" I know she's aware of what we do, but I can't deprogram nor will I ever confirm.

She just nods and picks up her fork before diving in. With what my dad told me about his father, I'm not surprised. I also know we will never know the full extent, but I think we are going to need to investigate all areas now. My train of thought stops when I hear her moans. When I look at her, her face is an inch from the plate as she inhales the pasta.

Why do so many men like women who only eat salads? She finishes the plate in less time than it took to find her, which isn't saying much. I'm about to give her my plate when she gets up and runs. I rush into the bathroom to follow her as she empties her stomach. I didn't try it, but nobody would poison the entire household nor would poison work this fast.

"What's wrong? What can I do?" I drop behind her and grab her hair while texting the doctor to get to my dad's house immediately. She doesn't say anything as she leans against the wall for strength.

We stay together until the doctor comes to the house. He is the only non-family member to have access to all our residences for obvious reasons. I gave him directions so he found us quickly. "What's going on?"

I point to Dani who is still puking and give him the rundown. He goes and sniffs my plate of food before coming back. "Anything she can't eat?"

"Dairy." It sounds pained coming out. I grab her a glass of water, but I don't know if that would help. I hand it over after the doctor nods.

"Well, you just ate a bunch, so this is probably going to be all night. Let me set you up with an IV so you don't get dehydrated. What room do you want to be in?" He waits until I answer to get the stuff from his car. I carry her to the bedroom, so she'll be comfortable. As soon as her feet touch the floor, she leaves for another room. I follow her because what the hell?

"What's wrong with the other room?"

"I'm not keeping you up all night. You don't need to see this." She tries to shut the door in my face, but I leave my foot there. "Move your foot before I try out the gun your dad gave me."

I smirk. My dad wouldn't give her a gun. "I'm staying with you. Wherever that is." My face falls. "Why did he give you that?" At least the doctor is close if she does shoot me.

"When you're grumpy in the morning, it's on you. He wanted me to be able to protect myself." She pushes me away and goes into the first bedroom. "Can you sleep on the other side tonight?"

At least we are sharing the bed. I grab all my weapons from the nightstand so I can place them on the other one right when doc walks in. "Alright, miss. I just need your arm and I'll get this set up in no time. Tony, you remember how to do this right?" I nod. After getting my first one, I learned how to get rid of it. "I'm going to leave another bag for the morning after you wake up. I've added antinausea medicine into this one."

I watch as he sets everything up and lightly lifts her arm. I wasn't expecting her to flinch when the needle got close. If someone is getting an IV, they are usually out. This is my first time watching a conscious person get one.

"You don't have to look so mad. I'll be fine once it gets out of my system." She pulls her arm from doc and runs into the bathroom. He didn't connect her, but he did line.

"I'll handle the rest." He hesitates, which is unlike him. When he's dismissed, he usually disappears faster than he arrived. "What."

He looks between the bathroom and me. "That sauce has a lot of dairy in it. How did it get into her system?"

And he makes me feel worse. I don't know what ingredients are in things. If they taste good, I eat it and grab leftovers. If it doesn't, I finish my plate and say I have stuff at home. A very important Italian rule, never, under any circumstances say you don't like the food. Unless you want to be impaled with any kitchen utensil. "I didn't know."

"Ask for ingredients next time. I have a feeling she won't be eating for the rest of the week. Let me know if you need me back." This time, he leaves.

I pull the pole into the bathroom and attach it to her, while she leans against the wall. I leave her alone in the bathroom and get ready for bed. I run to the kitchen to get waters, tea, and crackers, but I have a feeling nothing will be touched.

When I get back to the room, her eyes are closed, but she's still next to the toilet. I set up a make shift bed with blankets and pillows before laying down. She's right, I'm not going to get any sleep and not for the reason I hoped for.

Chapter 15

Daniella

It's been a week of Hell. Honestly, Hell would probably have been more preferred. Tony gave me that pasta not knowing I couldn't eat it. Not that I thought to ask. Then, I was out of it for two days before my period came. So, Tony thought I was still sick due to the pasta and wanted to call the doctor back. I refused, almost shot him. His dad took my side. Now, this entire house is a powder keg waiting to explode. Oh, and I haven't told Mr. Segreto the great news. His father started the whole problem with Hal.

Matteo is pissed because he's dealing with Tony's responsibilities while Tony is stuck here. Oh, and everyone, I mean everyone, is invested in my relationship with Tony.

When I went back to Tony's place after that first night, I figured we'd be here for a week, not longer, so I didn't grab everything I should have. Want to watch a made man squirm? Tell him to pick up feminine products. Maria, who runs the house, was kind enough to get me what I needed. At least she knew what I was talking about.

I made my way to the kitchen, where all the boys are talking in Italian. For some reason they stop once I enter. "Don't mind me. I'm just grabbing safe food. Then, I'll be gone. It's not like I understand." Have I been sassier than normal? Yes. Do they deserve my attitude? Also, yes. Before the whole pasta fiasco, I was treated normally. Now, it's like I'm going to break if I do anything. I pick up the plate that has my name on it. Maria has been kind enough to adjust a meal for me. She goes one step above by marking it so nobody, except me, touches it.

"Are you sure that's safe?" "Should I try it?" "I'll carry it for you." Exhibit a.

"Boys!" I can't take it anymore. They all appear frozen. I doubt anyone has ever yelled at them, but I'm done. "I'm here to be nice. I have no problem packing my things and leaving. I have no issue living alone without 'protection', there are other ways to get pleasure, and I can make sure to honor my brother without living here. You all need to calm down." The funny thing about telling someone to calm down, it does the opposite.

"Calm down? Calm down? Have you lost your mind? You do not come into my home and insult me like that. Do you know who I am? You might be a female, but I can hand you over to whoever has a hit on you and take the money for myself!"

Huh. I wasn't expecting the first outburst to be by Mr. Segreto. "Really? I came into your house? *You* invited me and then locked me inside. I'm not one of *your* soldiers who will jump off a bridge if *you* say to. I'm the one saving your ass by dealing with problems *your* father caused. If you wanted the money, you would have killed me, but you don't need the money." I start to leave, but stop at the doorway. "We are going to sit down tonight for dinner and have a civilized conversation. So, you have about four hours to get your heads on."

I leave them staring after me. Maybe I was too hard on them, but I will not be a wall flower.

***

I ate lunch in the office I have taken over. I finished all the procedures to give to Mr. Segreto. One nice thing about them acting weird, I'm getting work done. Tony, Mr. Segreto and I all work from different offices during the day and I get Tony to myself at night. Each night, we get ready for bed together before he pulls me half on top of him so we can sleep. Each morning, I wake up on the opposite side and him on his stomach.

I don't mind, but I want something more. We haven't had sex since the first night, maybe it was morning, whenever. First, my stomach, then my period, but now, it's just weird being under the same roof as his father. We are also sleeping in Tony's childhood bedroom. It's been updated, but I can't look past certain things. I didn't bring the condoms and he never asked. I wonder if it's because I'm covered.

I grab my notebook with the topics we need to discuss at dinner and go get ready. I asked Maria for something simple tonight, which she was more than happy about. Apparently, they like fancy more than every once in a while. Tonight is just the four of us while I give them an update.

Mr. Segreto asked me to handle a meeting with one of guys suspected of trying to kill Tony, so I got to have a little fun while also learning who the mastermind is. Mr. Segreto expects us to be in the clear after only one more night here. Tony was pissed he had to stay home while I had fun, but when I told him what I learned, his tune slightly changed. Apparently, they didn't think he would give us any information.

I thought I'd be the first, but Tony is already seated. "Good, I'm hoping we can talk before my dad arrives." I nod. We always have a breakdown of our day while trying to fall asleep. "Did I do something to hurt you?" I shake my head. Unsure where this is coming from or going. "Why haven't you touched me or kissed me since that first night? I can't think of anything other than I did something."

I put my hand on his to stop his rambling. He is always so confident, but with me, it's like a giraffe trying to take its first steps. "You did nothing. It's just weird being under the same roof as your dad. In his house. With his rules." He looks more confused, so I power on. "Also, I was either sick, on my period, or out on assignment since that night."

That snaps something in him. "I have no issue doing whatever I please in my bedroom. I have never brought a girl here and slept with someone in that bedroom. My dad doesn't care. We are consenting adults."

"What don't I care about?" Mr. Segreto asks. This is why I wait until we are behind closed doors to discuss sensitive items. I never had *the talk* with my parents. They were gone before I could hear it. Alex was terrified of me having any questions, so we didn't talk about it.

"Nothing." "Us having sex under your roof." I say at the same time Tony speaks.

"You are both consenting adults, but I'd prefer not to be here when anything occurs. Also, I'm in the other wing, so I wouldn't hear anything." I blink while Tony smirks. This is so weird.

Matteo walks in at the tail end of Mr. Segreto's answer. "Is it time to eat or are we going to have the talk again?" I don't like being triple teamed, but I must admit they make me feel like I'm part of the family even though I'm not. I like the banter even if the jokes are a lot darker than what Alex and I would do.

"No. Let's eat before the food gets cold. I have a few things on my list and then we can all go to bed. Hopefully, tomorrow will be the last night we are stuck here. Not that it hasn't been nice." I start passing the food while I'm talking.

The three of them put food on their plate, but they don't eat it. I freeze with my fork halfway to my mouth. "What's wrong?" Oh no, someone can't eat this. After all the meals they tried to destroy me with, I pick the one they can't eat.

"Nothing." They all say quickly and at the same time. But none of them start eating. I know they don't say grace before eating. Maybe I broke some unspoken rule? I put my fork down and look at all of them.

"What is this?" Mr. Segreto asks, while pushing the food around.

"Goulash. Without the cheese. Obviously. But, here's the bowl of cheese if you want to mix it in." I pass him the bowl thinking that will help. Nope, they keep staring at their plates, which are more like fancy soup plate bowl things. "It's similar to stew, but not as soupy."

Still nothing. Alright, if they won't start eating, I will. I dig in to my meal and grab a roll to help suck up some of the liquid so it doesn't make too much of a mess. I told Maria I would clean up.

I'm finished and they haven't even started. I guess I'll start going through my notes, while they contemplate eating the meal I had made. I'm about to finish with my last point, which is how to integrate all the changes seamlessly. "It's not going to kill you. It's not poisoned." They still won't budge.

Instead of forcing them to eat something new, which isn't that far from what we usually have. I go back to the kitchen, grab three bowls, three spoons, milk, and a box of cereal. If they want to act weird, so be it.

I place everything on the table. "Well, I think the best way to get all these changes up and running would be to have a corporate wide accounting training session for anyone that works in accounting or deals directly with them. We should have it over two days. The first to talk with the accounting team to make sure everything is easy and accepted before sharing with the non-accounting folk that will be impacted."

I get murmurs of agreement, but nothing else. Sighing, I get up and start cleaning. I take the serving bowl and put it into individual containers. Clean my dishes. The men are still looking at their bowls and the cereal is still sitting there. I put the milk away, but the rest they can handle. With their weirdness, I go upstairs.

***

I'm in my pajamas with a book when Tony finally comes up. He doesn't say anything and goes straight to the closet. When he comes out, he's dressed in a suit. "It's bedtime, not go out. Especially when your father has you on house arrest." I feel like all I've done today is state the obvious.

"I want you to dance with me." Great, it's turning into the weirdest night. First the conversation about sex with his dad. Then them not touching the dinner. Now this.

"Why?" I'm comfy. I don't want to get up, nor do I want to dance in my pjs.

Instead of answering me, he comes over to my side of the bed and picks me up. I know I'm not the lightest thing, but he makes me feel petite. He places me on my feet and begins dancing with me. I could fall asleep like this. We need to add this to our nightly ritual. I have never felt the world wash away quite so quickly.

"We were surprised about the meal. It was a staple growing up. My dad actually made it. It was the only thing he could put together. Plus, it made a ton of leftovers." He voice is barely above a whisper, but the fact that it wasn't the food, but the memories, makes me happy. At least I didn't destroy our relationship.

"You have great ideas and dad wants to hire you full-time to manage the accounting aspects. I think he wants to keep you close and safe more than anything."

I gasp. I want to stay on. This is the first place that I've worked at that I actually feel like I'm making a difference. It comes with really nice benefits too, like the boss's son.

"More importantly, I want you to move in with me. Permanently. I don't want to force you to stay which is what keeps happening. It's your choice, but."

He leaves the choice hanging. Either his place or mine, I doubt we won't be sharing the same bed ever. "Is your place safe enough for you?"

He stops the swaying. "Seriously? Is that a yes?" His eyes are brighter than they've been in a while. I can't stop myself, I nod. "We can get a new place if you want. I'll look into houses." He tries to get out of my grip.

"Maybe we can just put a little lobby into the penthouse so the elevator isn't the door. I think looking at houses is a tad too much, too fast." I keep him in my grip and resume the swaying. This time at a much slower pace.

"Can I kiss you?" He's back to that soft voice. When I look up at him, I can feel his need. Instead of answering with words, I kiss him. Gently before letting it spiral. I swear every time I try to go slow, a hunger in me comes out and I can't get enough of him.

Everything turns needy. Lips, hands, bodies. Our lips stay locked, while our hands start exploring. My body is melting into him. I need his clothes off, but his suit is pristine. I don't want to wrinkle it. I try to pull back, but his hand is behind my head keeping us close. I put my hands on his chest, so he knows I need a second.

As soon as my lips are off his, they want more, but I let my brain take control before my body is running the show. I guide him back to the bed and push him down so he's sitting on the edge. First, I take his jacket and vest and place them on the chair. Next, his shirt, this is don't care about as much. With every button undone, he gets a kiss placed where that button hid his body from me. Next, his shoes and socks, which land with his shirt. Finally, his pants, he helps by lifting his hips after I unbutton them. I'm in complete control, which I think is new for him. I place the pants with the jacket and vest.

Before he can pull me into him, I drop to my knees. He doesn't resist as I pull his briefs down so I can take his hard length into my mouth. I focus on the tip. Swirling my tongue as I left my hand slide up and down. As soon as I taste him, I realize my mistake. I'm never going to get enough of him.

I kiss the underside to make it easier when I swallow him whole. I had a full dinner, but I'm ready for dessert. As I take him into my mouth, I have my first thought of horror. He's not going to fit. I knew he was large; I still don't know how he fit inside me when we had sex. But this. I have a small mouth. He starts rubbing the back of my neck, relaxing me as I take him deeper.

I can feel he's close, so I do the one thing that will push him over the edge, I leave one hand on what I can't fit and let the other start massaging his balls. I feel him tense as he shoots his cum down my throat. I follow his motions and keep him inside until I feel him still.

Chapter 16

Tony

I can't move. I've never come that hard, that quickly, with a blow job. I want to repay the favor, but she dresses me in a pair of pajama pants and rests her head on my chest. I want to see how wet she is. Before I know it, she's asleep and I'm drifting off to the feel of her breathing.

The past week has been rough. She hasn't been sleeping in here for some reason. She's been awake when we wake up and after we turn in. The one night, I stayed awake as long as possible and fell asleep on the couch. When I woke up after the movie ended, she was still up. Without her in here, I haven't been sleeping well. Tossing and turning all night. Waking up tired. Nothing worked.

Now that she's back in my bed, I realize she was the missing part. I squeeze her closer to me and that's when I hear it. She's whimpering. She never did that before. Not that I had a lot of experience sleeping next to her before we got moved. I run my hand along her back since she always likes that. It works, she stopped moving. I relax now that's she back to sleeping.

It was only a breath and instead of moving, she's crying. I need to stop this. "Mostriciattola, you need to wake up." I keep saying her name and that's she safe, but it seems to be making matters worse. She's locked into this dream and I can't help her. I pull her into my lap, but that doesn't work. I start rocking her. Babies like that? Well, I don't because I feel seasick.

This is going to be weird, but I know who can handle this. "Dad. How quickly can you come to my room? Dani won't wake up."

"I'll be right there." He hangs up the phone. I guess he hasn't been sleeping either. He picked up on the first ring, but I think it's her that has him moving fast. He barges into the room. "What's wrong."

"She won't wake up. She started whimpering, then crying. I don't know what to do." I'm sitting against the headboard, so he can fully see her where he's standing.

"How often does she…" he trails off while watching her cycle through the whimpering, then crying. Only this time, after she cries, she stiffens and shoots up. I can tell she's disoriented, but my dad can't.

He steps towards us seeming to relax. Dani launches off me and starts choking him. He stumbles, caught off guard and that's all she needed. She has him pinned to the floor with her tiny hands around his neck. In any other scenario, I would laugh. The small accountant just took down one of the five bosses in New York.

I grab her around the waist and lift her straight off him. That's when she decides to try to head butt me. "Take me. Just leave him alone!" I drop her. I was not expecting her to make that loud of a noise. My right ear is ringing, which happens when I shoot, but this is worse.

"Shhhh. Nobody is taking anyone. We are all safe." Well, my dad might kill her for trying to kill him, but I'll leave that out. "Who was I trying to take instead of you?" My dad asks while I'm trying to soothe her.

I send daggers his way. Now is not the time for questions, even though I want to know. I hate to admit this, but I think my dad's question pulled her out more than my soothing. At least I was right with knowing he would know how to get her out of the nightmare. "Do you want to talk about it?" Dad's sending those same daggers back.

"Sorry I woke you both. I'll just go to another room." She goes to leave, but my dad closes the door before she can get a finger out.

"No. We either discuss this now or we do this the difficult way. I have no problem forcing answers out of you, but my son would object." My dad lays into her. He's never this aggressive even when dealing with problem people. "Who were you trying to protect? Who was he?"

I see her sigh since I still can't hear. She knows this isn't like the warehouse. He will get the answers he wants. I want. She looks at him. It's the same look she gives me when she's trying to figure out the best way to handle something or when she is reading me. "Not here. Not with him." She forces the door open and follows him.

I go to follow, but she shut the door behind her. When the door doesn't budge, I realize they jammed it so I wouldn't follow.

***

When I finally gave up trying to open the door, I realized how tired I truly am. I came up hours ago and have a few meetings scheduled in less than five hours. I decide to give sleep a try and quickly pass out.

I went to bed with one woman on top of me and planned to wake her how she'd helped get me relaxed enough to sleep. However, she left with my father and neither of them have unjammed my door. I called both of them, found Dani's phone, and then tried my father's favorite men. Nobody is responding. There is only one person that can help.

"Do you have any idea what time it is? I'm doing your job while you're on house arrest with dad. I need sleep. I don't want to listen to your sad stories about how Dani won't love you or whatever."

Well, at least he answered. "They locked me in my room. Can you please get me out of here? I have meetings and if I don't attend, you are going to have more of my duties to managed."

There's no answer. Maybe I'm in a dead zone? My phone has full bars and the call didn't drop. Maybe he is? That would usually drop the call too though. My pre-coffee brain isn't functioning. "You called me. At the crack of dawn because dad locked you in."

I guess he was processing. Maybe I should offer coffee. "He didn't lock me in. I can pick a lock. He jammed the door shut and I am not jumping out the third story window. So don't suggest that."

"Fine. Give me an hour. Do you want to grace the office with your presence today? I'm picking up breakfast and coffee on my way after I take a shower. Text me your order." At least he's getting food and coffee.

Since he suggested it, I think I will go in the office. I haven't been in for a while not that anyone is complaining. When the boss's son tells you he has to work from home, nobody questions it.

After a shower, I get a new suit. Part of me wants to wear the one I put on to dance with Dani, but I want to save that suit for special occasions. Going into the office isn't one of them. Unless she's also in the office and I can have her on my desk for lunch. If he's going to be an hour, I might as well shower and tidy up my room. I tried to empty her bags into drawers, but she didn't like that so everything has been half in a bag or thrown in neat piles on the floor.

I'm cleanly shaven, showered, dressed, my room is clean, and my bag is packed. I'm bursting at the seams to get out of this room. Thankfully, Matty showed up with food and coffee before escorting me to the driveway. I guess I'm not in the clear because we have a driver.

In different times, soldiers have driven us places for added security, but I hate it. I'd rather have some control by being behind the wheel. Sitting as a passenger, I can't do anything. I can shoot, but there are typically too many innocents or cameras to safely pull that off. The car is bullet-proofed, so I'm not worried I'll get shot.

We pull into the parking garage in time for me to make it to my meetings. After letting them check the areas, I rush to the elevators. Just because they checked doesn't mean someone can't try something. Nothing has changed. The office still looks the same, people are the same. Two are clearly missing, but nobody else seems to mind.

When my dad is here, everyone is on their game. When he isn't, everyone is still on their game, but the atmosphere is much more relaxed. Work still gets done since he is still working, just not here. He hates being in the office. I'm the same way. I love getting work done and sometimes it is harder with so many people. A walk for coffee might take ten minutes instead of one. Bathroom breaks turn into chit chat. Lunch becomes causal.

I will admit in person meetings are more beneficial. I don't have to worry about lag time. I can see faces to make sure they actually understand what's being said. People are braver at asking questions because they know they have my attention fully. The back-to-back-to-back meetings go smoothly.

I finish up a few administrative things before I'm ready to go. It's hard to work without your computer. Mine happens to be at my father's. I stop at Matteo's office to see what his plans are. For the first time, his door is shut. I jiggle the handle and it's locked. I can't hear anything. We made sure our three offices were almost completely soundproof.

I knock and wait.

I hear his response.

He's safe. When we were younger and our parents were fighting, we created a signal to let each other know we were good. It stuck with us and has gotten us out of a few incidents.

I turn and nod to the guy that drove us and followed up here. All the employees are used to seeing soldiers in and out of here daily. Usually, they come for a meeting before leaving. They don't linger, but that's his job today.

The elevator door opens to the parking garage. I take a look around before stepping out. The soldier remains a step behind me. I hear it before it hits me.

I feel the tearing of my skin. I know I've been shot. There isn't anything that compares to it. I fall into the elevator, which is good, but the soldier is no longer behind me.

Screw it. I use my card and scan it. The elevator slams shut before an express trip to our office. The elevator opens and closes all day, so nobody notices it. I pull my phone out, but it slips out of my grasp.

The hand I was using to put pressure on the wound is numb. That's not good.

I feel myself start to drift off. I call Linda. Our office magician. She handles everything and keeps all the companies running. She is also married to my dad's original enforcer, so blood doesn't bother her.

"Hi sweetie. What can I help you with?" She is such a mother to everyone. Even the men much older than her.

"Elevator. Call dad. Matteo. Shot." The phone disconnects before I get the words out.

When the door to the elevator opens, I see her face right before everything goes dark. A smell jerks me up. Linda is still there. "Eyes on me. Where did this happen?" I get the smell again.

"Park." I can't get the words out. The last few times I was shot, this didn't happen. They were easily fixed by doc. He should be able to patch me right back up.

***

The smells aren't quite right, but everything else is perfect. We're in dad's kitchen and I'm teaching Dani how to make the sauce. It's a family secret that we don't have written down anywhere. It's also the only thing I can make.

The temperature is a tad colder than usual, but being near the stove helps. Now that we are just simmering the sauce, I put Dani on the counter. Dad and Matteo are away, so we have the entire house to ourselves. I plan to use the entirety of the house to make her happy.

We can't leave the kitchen until the sauce is finished, so I plant myself between her legs and kiss her. I can hear the sauce popping, which is perfect. I let myself get lost in the sweet taste of her lips, which she opens immediately. Tonight is about exploring though, there is no rush. I plan on making sure every inch of her is tasted and explored before we finally go to sleep.

She squeezes her legs around my waist, pulling me closer. She's done that before when she wants to speed things up.

But the problem isn't the action. It's the pain. Something is wrong.

I pull back and hear her groan. Then I see my side is bleeding. I shouldn't be able to see the blood since I wear black all the time. Black always hides the blood stains. Why aren't I wearing block?

Dani notices the blood, but she isn't panicking. Why isn't she?

"Tony, don't worry. It'll all be over soon." She leans back in and

111

kisses me, but this time, it isn't sweet and tempting. This is hard and punishing. Usually, I like that. Right now? I can't stand it.

The pot starts to boil over. The sauce spraying the ceiling. I quickly return my focus to the stove, but the sauce is gone, the stove is off. I look over my shoulder and Dani is gone.

***

I try to sit upright. I can't. My hands are restrained to the side of the bed. My legs aren't moving. All I hear is the beeping, which keeps increasing. It's too bright. I never sleep with lights on. Hell, I barely have them on any other time.

"You shouldn't be awake already. How are you feeling? Can I get you something?" I don't know this woman, but she is speaking in hushed tones. I look around the room and find out why. Curled in a ball on a chair is Dani.

Outside the door, Mario, one of my soldiers has his phone to his ear. But he's staring at me. Not with anger or pity, but relief. He's also not forcibly removing this woman, so she's fine, I guess.

"What happened?" As soon as the words are out of my mouth, images come rushing back in. The office, the elevator, parking garage, the soldier, blood, Linda, darkness. "Never mind. No pain meds. I can't."

The nurse doesn't say anything, but her face speaks volume. I'm insane for not taking pain medication after getting shot. I did the first time and I swore I would never have any ever again. The pain is manageable. I'll heal. Quickly, I hope. I have plans for someone.

"Your father left an hour ago, but we're letting him know you are awake. Can I get either of you anything?" This comes from Mario. My dad wouldn't leave just a soldier in the hospital. The fact that he left means something big is going on.

"Coffee. Please. Maybe a sandwich?" I don't remember the last time I ate or drank. "What day is it?" Maybe that will help me out.

Chapter 17

Daniella

I couldn't answer Mr. Segreto's questions in front of Tony. He is stressed out enough without me adding on all my fears. I follow Mr. S into his office. He sits on the giant desk instead of behind it. I've never been in Mr. S's office. This is one of the places I never wanted to see. From what I've heard, the boss's office is the most sacred places in the entire family. Only the boss can sit behind the desk. Only people of extreme importance are allowed on the other side. Fuck, you can't be in here without the boss. Or so I've been told.

He realizes I won't speak without prompts. "Go ahead. What couldn't you say in front of my son?"

"He's the him. I watch him get shot and they take him. I don't know who they are. But after I *talked* with that last group, the dreams started." I don't want him to know about my dream beliefs. I can tell you the significance of seemingly random items in your dream. Why recurrent dreams occur and their meaning. Why certain times dreams are more lucid.

Well, I can't say why this dream paralyzes me. Literally. The first time I had the dream, I tried to wake myself only to be panicking because I was unable to move anything except my eyes. When the tears started, I could open my mouth, but no sounds came out. It was only to get air in and out. So, I've done the smartest thing possible. I haven't been sleeping. Can't have nightmares if you aren't asleep.

Tonight though, I did something I've never done before. I feel asleep as soon as my head hit the pillow, or chest of Tony. Same thing really. Well, my pillow is typically not as firm. I hoped the quickness of falling asleep was because I was so exhausted that the dream couldn't get me. I was wrong. Only this time, it was so much worse. Tony witnessed it. His dad witnessed it. I'm going to have to leave the country. Luckily, Matteo wasn't here.

"Do you want me to have doc prescribe something to let you sleep?" That would be the smart thing to do.

"Can he guarantee that the dream won't get me there?" I see his face tighten. "That's what I thought. I just need to get the people trying to hurt him, so I know he's safe."

"Then what? We aren't in the safest business. This isn't the first time someone has tried to kill a member of my family and I doubt it will be the last. So. What are you going to do about it?" He challenges.

I want to take Tony far away and keep him safe and away from harm. I also can't make him leave his family. I know how precious this time together is no matter how much time they have together. I thought I would have my entire life, but that was taken from me like their last breaths. "When you have an answer, let me know. For now, let's get the doctor to check you out and then hopefully, you can get back to sleep."

There is no point arguing. I've tried and failed at getting the doctor not to investigate me, but maybe he'll have something that can help. I doubt my anxiety will let it though. "Can you please keep this between us? I don't want him to worry any more than he already has been."

***

After the doctor verified he couldn't do anything and I needed sleep, he gave me something and I was out. Happily in the spare room I claimed and not with Tony. He doesn't need to see this again.

When I woke up, I realized I missed the entire morning, but no nightmares followed me. After getting ready quickly in lounge wear since I'm not going into the office, I found the most important thing. Coffee. Maria offered to not only make me lunch, but fill me in on the family gossip. I was never into reality tv shows because of the gossip, but made men apparently gossip more according to Maria. She told me everything about their relationships, territories, best food places that are safe. Nothing illegal, nothing dangerous in anyone's hands. But I have a feeling she was just happy to have another female around.

I decided to check in on Mr. S since Tony went into the office today before I hunkered down in my office. I raised my hand to knock on the open door, but stopped. Something was wrong. Mr. Segreto's eyes locked on mine. I knew what had happened before he said a single word.

My nightmare has come true.

"Where are you taking him? Is that the best place? No, I don't care about that. What about Matty? Put him on. What happened. Details. We're coming." He slides his phone into his pocket, but I'm already running. He will not lock me inside. If Tony is hurt, I'm checking on him myself.

***

The ride to the hospital is tense. Mr. Segreto keeps checking on me. I'm fairly sure I should be the one checking on him.

His son was shot. His son is on the way to the hospital. His son has a hit on him. Ok, I have that too, but still. I might need to be admitted too if I can't start thinking rationally. I'm already panicking, but I know the one thing that will help. Too bad I don't have my bag. Or my phone. I wasn't thinking clearly enough to grab stuff before I was moving to his car.

I start checking the center console, nothing. The glove box has some napkins and a pen. I can make this work. I count the napkins to know how many lists I'll have to fit on each.

Questions to ask the hospital staff; food locations nearby (since I can't google); questions for his guard; questions for the shooter; ideas for how to figure out how the shooter knew he'd be in the office today. I let myself get lost in the lists. Mr. Segreto's phone keeps ringing through the audio system so I try my best not to listen so he has some privacy. Plus, I will have plausible deniability.

Did you know hospitals have valet? Well, they do when you are the head of a crime family. You also get VIP treatment, go through the ambulance entrance. Yeah, nothing seems fair when you think about it, but I'll worry about that later. I don't need to ask where to go. I follow the stream of well-dressed then very well-dressed men to the door of a room.

"Who are you?" As I burst through the doors. "Ah, sorry sir. Your son is right here. We are getting ready to take him up for surgery to remove the bullet and fix any internal damage."

"Look doctor, I don't know you. I want my doc to be allowed full rights and to scrub in. He's on his way, but I don't want you to wait for him. Just know, if anything happens to my son on your table, you will not like the outcome. Also, I get the bullet. The only people touching it are you, my doc, and me." He doesn't allow the doctor to get a word in before he makes his way to the foot of Tony's bed.

He's unconscious and pale. His clothes are cut everywhere. I check his vitals, which look fine? I don't really know enough about trauma and vitals. I know what normal vitals are. I go over to his side and kiss his forehead, like he always does to me. Without another word I turn and leave.

I head back towards the exit, but Matteo is charging forward. His dad might kill him or he might just lose himself for letting something happen to Tony. Grabbing his arm, he stops when I don't let go. "You're driving. Let's go." When he doesn't follow, I pull on his arm and drag him. "Now."

***

The eerie calm has settled over me. I know what needs to happen. The panic is on the back burner. I can't help him while he's in surgery, so I left him with the doctors and his father who was issuing threats. Mr. S might not know medicine, but he can persuade them.

"Where am I taking us?" This is the first thing he's said since I snatched him.

I look at him. I can see the worry etched in his face. So similar to Tony, but still so different. "First, we are getting the soldier who allowed him to get shot. Second, we are getting my tips for finding the shooter to your tech wizard. Third, I'm going to make the guy wish he never got into the elevator with Tony and allowed this to happen. Fourth, you get your turn and your father, if he wants one. Finally, I'm going to hunt and harm the shooter."

His mouth is stuck open. No longer watching the traffic light that was red. I guess he doesn't hear the horns. "Drive." Honestly, you'd think I said something crazy.

My tone snaps him out of it. "When did you come up with that list?" That's not what I would've asked first.

"On the drive to the hospital. Sadly, I left my phone and bag at your dad's, so I had to use napkins." I pull them out. "I have everything ready to go. I just need a little help on some items. But I think people will be happy to have a task while we wait for an update."

He's about to respond when his phone rings and he answers it right away. I see the name on the screen, so it's not shocking. "Where are you. Have you seen Dani? One second, she was here, the next gone."

That's sweet, he's worried about me. "We're together Mr. S. Matty is helping me accomplish a few tasks, but we will be back before Tony wakes up from surgery."

"You are not allowed to run off like that! I can't believe you. I'm assigning two men to be your shadows."

"Dad. We're fine. There are two cars trailing us since the hospital. I'll be calling Sam for help with hunting."

We can hear his sigh. Is it relief or disbelief? "Do not lose your tails. That's an order. Take me off speaker." I can hear his muffled voice, but nothing specific. Matteo only grunts or gives one-word answers. Nothing I can understand. He hangs up the phone and ignores the address I put in the navigation system.

"Dad got us a present. Once we arrive, I'm going to reach out to Sam, but I need you to wait in the car until we know it's safe." Now it's my turn to groan. I hate the waiting rule. I get it, but still.

We pull in front of a familiar building. I've never been here, but it looks just like Tony's warehouse. I wait for what feels like an hour. I don't like sitting still. The fact that I allowed him to drive was testing my patience.

When my door opens, I jump out and compose myself before storming the warehouse. I would have brought my new gun since I'm hunting one soldier and another person unafraid of the wrath of one of the most powerful men in New York.

Someone is tied to the chair. The closer I get, the more I see. His left eye is swollen shut. I don't know if he's sleeping or unconscious. I kick his leg. Not too hard. Just enough to wake him. I hear a muffled groan. If someone broke his jaw, I'm not going to get any answers.

His right eye opens and he tries to sit up. I can tell he hasn't heard of me. The men in this family who have heard, well, they are typically giving me a long once-over before looking like they are trying to figure out the puzzle.

"Hi. I'm Dani. What's your name? What can I call you?" He tries to talk, but no sound comes out. "Can you write?" He nods. "Good to know."

I pull up a chair and sit as close as possible without him being able to touch me. "Let's start with some simple questions. Do you know why you're here?" Yes. "Do you regret what you did?" Yes. "Were you paid to not go first?" He freezes. I don't know if he's a mole or worse, but that leaves me with less questions. "You are going to write the name of who paid you. The amount you were paid. After I have the information verified, we'll talk more. But while I wait, I'm going to let someone else deal with their anger. So, it's in your best interest not to lie."

When his hand is untied, he writes all the information, but this talk didn't help. "Hang him up." I hand the paper to Mario, my new shadow, also one of the men I've seen at Tony's warehouse. I was told he's liked by everyone. His mom owns a bagel and pizza shop that is legit that everyone loves. So, if you want good service, you need to butter up Mario.

Once he's hanging by his hands, I go to the tools. Not as fun as Tony's, but I can make do. I quickly find all the tools to be quite fun, but my favorite: the whip. This one has a feather on one side and a blade on the other. You can't tell what will hit him each time.

When the information comes back correct, I let Matteo take his guilt out on him and I leave with my shadows.

***

After a quick shower. New clothes. My bag. I pack some necessities for Tony before letting my shadows take me back to the hospital. Tony hasn't woken yet, but it's got to be soon? The doctors said it was normal. Mr. Segreto was shocked when I texted him all the questions and told him to either take notes or record the conversation.

When we arrive, I'm escorted to a different room. It's quieter. I make sure to meet his nurses and get a quick update. I haven't slept. The last time I slept without medicine, the nightmare came true. I don't know what I'll see the next time I close my eyes.

I settle into the chair next to the bed and curl up as best as possible. I don't want to make too much noise. As much as I want to see his piercing eyes, I want him to rest if that's what his body needs to recover.

I don't mean to drift off, but I can't help it. No nightmares find me. It's almost like my brain knows I need something better. I dream of helping Tony recover. From sponge baths to helping him get ready to helping with other needs.

The smell of coffee pulls me back to consciousness. When I open my eyes, I catch Tony staring at me. He has a sandwich on the tray, but it only looks like he took one bite. Now, I'm hungry and ready for coffee, but I won't steal his food. I made sure to send the shadows on a snack packing mission while I showered.

I quickly untangle myself from the blanket that's on me. No idea where that came from. I look at his vitals, all within normal range of a normal person. Not one that was shot. "How do you feel? Do you need anything?"

Chapter 18

Tony

I'm sitting in bed watching Dani sleep. Mario brought me a sandwich and coffee. I tried the sandwich, but it's too much too quickly. I have a feeling soup will be my friend. The first bite I had to spit out. Mario thought something was wrong with it, but the nurse swept in and brought gelatin and soup. A weird combination, but I don't care

I have never seen Dani sleep this long. Usually, I'm her pillow and even though she falls asleep first, I'm close behind. In the morning, she's awake and moving by the time my alarm goes off. She has never set one, which I find weird.

Since I have nothing better to do, I called dad and Matty. They want to come back, but I told them not to worry. The fact that they aren't here means they have things to handle.

Mario filled me in on what Daniella has been up to. Apparently, dad let her interrogate the soldier who let me get shot. He didn't pull the trigger, but he didn't follow a direct order. That's enough to warrant a trip to the warehouse. Usually it's just a beat down; this time, it's six feet.

I'm halfway through my coffee when her head snaps up. She's mid-stretch when our eyes lock. I should say something. Maybe let her know I'm in one piece and a bullet isn't going to stop me. Before I'm able to voice my thoughts, she's checking the monitor while fluffing my pillows.

When she lifts the gown, I freeze, Mario is standing at the door with another soldier, I shouldn't let her do what I hope she wants to do. Nope, not what I hoped for, she's checking my wound. Her fingers are cold against my skin, but they are soothing.

She scoffs when she sees that all of me woke up. Will dad let her give me a sponge bath? I should be able to convince him I don't need a nurse at the house. Shit. His house. We are never going to be allowed to leave and I don't think Dani will get over the "his roof, his rules" she made up in her mind. My dad couldn't care less.

"How are you feeling, mostriciattola?" I ask. Mario and the other capo cough into their hands when they hear my nickname for her. Usually, I keep it between us, but I don't think she knows what it means.

A look of incredulity crosses her face. Ahh, I love when her fire comes to play. "Me. You are asking me? You were shot! Why were you out of the house? You were under strict orders not to leave the property. But no. You had to go to the office for meetings? This is on you!"

I want to get out of bed to stop her pacing, but I know it's the only thing keeping her from tearing someone apart. Literally. "I had protection with me. It was just to the office for a few hours." Maybe, I should keep my mouth shut.

"Well, your protection is no longer adequate. You now have me with the three guys your dad stuck on me." She looks over at Mario. He's one of mine. That was smart on my father's part. I'll keep him on her forever. Or until he asks for a change, but I'm thinking he won't. Dani isn't a damsel. "Your father and Matteo are talking with the culprit. That's why they aren't here." She sits on the side of my bed. "How are you feeling?"

I want to touch her, but I know she goes from hot to cold quickly. I can't push. Based on her words, she was terrified. "I'm fine. A little sore, but nothing I can't handle." I push her hair out of her face. The fact she didn't notice it tells me she's worse than I thought. "Did you get enough sleep? I can have Mario take you home to rest."

And she's off. She's not speaking English, but it's also not Italian. I don't think I want the translation because I'm sure the beautiful words are not nice ones. "Mario, could you get us another round of coffees?" I should make her drink decaf, but that's not an option.

I watch Dani go to her bag and pull out her wallet and hand him cash. What. The. Hell. He smiles at her and walks away without taking any. He better get used to getting yelled at. Shockingly, she just frowns.

I woke up in an alternate reality. That's it! "I'm not leaving your side unless I have to. Doc was here and he said you can be discharged today. Pending you are able to get out of bed and have him stay at the house. Your father and I agreed, but only after the surgeon does another check."

She pulls out my clothes and places them on the bed. "Let's get you dressed so we can leave. I hate hospitals."

I wait until Mario comes back in the room with the coffees. I'm going to need to lean on someone and I might crush her.

***

Mario drove us to my father's, but we are still in the driveway. Two cars came with us. One in front and they are checking inside. The one in back is checking the perimeter. Nobody is stupid enough to attack my father's home though. But I let them do their job. It was a workout getting into the car and I don't know if I'll make it up the stairs to my room.

The ride was quiet since doc was in another car. "I had Matteo set up a room on the first floor closer to the kitchen and theater room. I figured the steps would be a lot and you need to rest a few days, at least, so movies. I also had snacks and soft foods added to the grocery list."

Where did she come from? If I wasn't already in love with her, I would be. On one hand, she is considerate and nurturing. The other hand, she's ready to torture and maim whoever harms her family. Hence her nickname. Mostriciattola. "I love you."

Whoops. Those weren't supposed to come out. I can't move. Why would I say that? I can't even blame the pain meds since they are out of my system. Or should be.

"All clear." The door opens to Mario. "What's wrong? Doc!"

"What happened?" My shirt is lifted. "No blood. Why are you both so pale?" He needs to stop talking, but he's checking our pulses. "Their hearts are racing." That's to himself.

"I need to check on the laundry." Dani bolts out the car and into the house. Nobody stops her, but they move away from her path.

Mario looks confused. "Should I follow her or help you? Do you even have a laundry room here?"

"I told her I loved her." Doc nods and leaves us. Mario just laughs. "Clearly, I caught her off guard."

"Dude. She might not say it, but she loves you too. You didn't witness what she accomplished in the warehouse. Let me just say, the men aren't giving her space because she's with you." He waits for me to swing out around before letting me lean on him.

Maria is in the foyer waiting to give me a hug and lets me know I'll be getting room service. It's a good thing Dani loves her because I don't think anyone else would be allowed in the room.

Once I'm settled in the new bedroom, I need to make sure she's safe. "Mario, can you find Daniella? I need a short break."

"Most likely in the boss's office, but I'll check." He turns to leave.

"What? Women aren't allowed in there. I never even saw my own mother in there." The look he gives me says I'm not wrong, but she is the first. I guess no break. I let him lead me to the one room I thought I knew all the rules for.

I hear her voice, and two more familiar ones the closer we get. Lucky for me, his office is on the first floor. Well, his main one that is. "Give me ten minutes with the guy and you'll have the answers." "Last time I let you in that building, I almost didn't get my fun." "You had more than enough answers though. I get results." "You don't get a say. You aren't made." "No shit. I'm a female. God forbid you let women into your ranks. If you did, it would not only run smoother, but the gossip chain wouldn't be so fast. I thought Real Housewives were dramatic, but these men are worse."

Great. Walking into an argument where she is making valid points is not going to be fun. I want her involved, but safe. I would never be able to be with someone I couldn't share my day with. Maybe that's why dad let's her in the office and warehouses. He knows I need her to be fine with it. Or it's because she brought us to the warehouse first.

"You are supposed to be in bed resting." Great, now my dad speaks. I guess Matteo and Dani were the two going for throats. It's oddly nice how much Matteo and Dani get along. I know they are safe with each other, but their bond is not because of me. I wonder how Alex would feel about Matteo having someone in his office the other day.

"I was planning to when I was told a female was permitted inside the office."

"It's a room, not the 'club'." Dani rolls her eyes at me. Like I'm not in the club. Nope, she is not allowed to be made. I know what it takes from you and I don't need that on her shoulders.

"We were just discussing some interview skills and felt Daniella might be helpful. She believes she can, so I will be taking her with me. Matteo will be staying here with you to make sure you don't leave or follow." Great, more orders.

If Mario wasn't here. Screw it. I've said crazier shit in the last hour. "I can call in to help. That way I'm safe and sound here, but still able to feel useful."

I can't let the two of them spend any more time together. They are mimicking facial expressions. I know that look far too well – I've lost my mind.

"Mario. You are with us. I'll take one other group. Doc and Maria will be here to keep an eye on both of you." My dad starts herding us out of the office. At least that rule remains. If he isn't inside, nobody is. Unless they want a bullet.

When we reach the theater room, Dani finally speaks. "I just need one minute with Tony and then I need to change before I'm ready. I like this outfit and after last time." She lets the sentence hang. Everyone else nods knowingly. What happened last time?

124

We step inside and she closes the door behind her. I want to move away from the door. She was right about the gossip chain in the families. I don't need this repeated. Whatever it is.

"I care about you. Is it love? I don't know. I've never felt it before. What I do know is I've never wanted to live like I do when I'm with you. When you got shot, it wasn't pretty. I don't want to feel like I've been shot when I know I wasn't. I don't want to feel your pain, but I do. I know you aren't ok. I know you are trying to act like this is fine and you'll be back in no time. But, with me, you don't have to lie. I don't want you to." She says all of this while changing.

I get it. I don't understand this feeling either, but my dad explained it to me. She doesn't have someone to explain it to her. Her brother might have shared stuff, but to what extent? We don't discuss feelings. That's not my family. I don't think it's her either. Instead of overthinking it. I kiss her.

Softly like in my dream before I found her this morning. I get lost in it. I don't let it spiral. She doesn't push us there either. It's sweet. It's better than words.

A knock on the door interrupts us. I don't want her to leave, but I also know it's the best option if my dad is agreeing. I kiss her once more before pulling away.

"Call me when you get there so I can watch." I say to her retreating form. The look the men give me make me think about how that really sounded.

***

Some movie is on. Neither of us are watching. Matteo is smiling at his phone. I want to ask, but I don't want to push him until he is ready.

My phone rings. I accept Mario's video call. "No recording." I don't want anyone to know what she's about to do. No, this is for me. Matteo looks at me and leaves the room.

I can barely hear her, but Mario knows better than to get too close. It could interfere with her plans. I recognize the guy since he shot me. But, I'm more interested in the whip she is holding. I remember her handcuffs, but I don't recall a whip. Our sex life just got a lot better. Not that we are having nearly enough.

"Where were we? Oh, you were going to tell me who gave you the instructions to shoot Tony." She's walking around him like he is nothing to be feared. I mean, he has more guns trained on him than he realizes and my father is there.

"I can't say. I'm not allowed to." He stutters. Even though she is running the show. His eyes are on my father.

I watch as Dani uses the whip a few times. A few more cuts into his skin than the first time I saw him. That's when it hits me. I know this man. I text Matteo who must not have gone far and mute my voice. "Isn't this Ivan's man?"

I pass him my phone. He doesn't look Russian, but most don't. At least, not Ivan's crew. Matteo nods. "Mario. Take me off video and hand me to my father."

"Yeah?" My dad is never nice on the phone. Maybe he realizes it too or he doesn't want this guy to know about how our family works.

"Ivan is behind this. That's his man." No goodbye. Nothing. The call ends as I hear screaming start.

"Why would the Russians want you dead?" That's a great question. We aren't at war with them anymore, but we don't invite them to social gatherings either. It's more of a mutual understanding that we all want to live.

Chapter 19

Daniella

So, the Russians want me dead? I thought it was the Irish, but that didn't make sense. I know who put the hit on me. Now I just need to figure out if I can kill them. Politics.

Mr. Segreto is about to get his fun, but I'm not done. With Tony off the phone, I can say certain things now. "Tony wasn't your target." That also made Mr. Segreto freeze. Mario is moving closer. I am his responsibility.

The man's face turns sheet white. When he saw Mr. Segreto, it paled, but this is a whole new level. "Interesting. I'm guessing you wanted to draw me out. Figured with him in the hospital, I might be reckless. Not the worst plan. You didn't anticipate me having the protection of the family though." I might be thinking out loud at this point, but his face tells me I'm spot on. "The question is why. Did your boss put the hit on me or did you guys just want the payout?"

When he doesn't answer, I walk away. Mr. Segreto looks ready to kill him. He wasn't happy with the man since he shot his son, but this is worse. I think changing my outfit didn't matter. "You have had a rough few days. Would you like a turn?" I put down my new favorite toy before looking at him.

He looks at his expensive shirt before frowning. He wasn't expecting to get dirty. "Mario. Would you mind giving Mr. Segreto the t-shirt under your sweater?" One benefit about being around all of men – they all know how to dress. I'm starting to think it's a class they have to take or something. Most wear suits, but Mario is slightly more causal. I think he prefers to blend in.

It takes a lot in me to keep my focus on the Russian instead of enjoying the show of changing shirts. I might not be watching, but he is. "Interesting. Does your boss know you prefer males?" Not that there isn't anything wrong with that, but I've found these families take traditional roles to the extreme.

"I don't know what you are talking. I like women." It comes out so quickly, it has to be rehearsed.

Nodding. "Of course, you do. I think if I strip naked right here, nothing would happen. But, if Mario does, well, something would."

"Do *not* strip!" Mr. Segreto growls. I give him a look to say I never would. That would be weird. I'm with his son not that that is a reason. More power to the women that can, but that's not something I'd be comfortable with.

Then a memory hits me. I stripped in the office after they locked me in the elevator. I'm going to need to talk to Tony about that.

A take a seat and pull out a chair for Mario. "Might as well take a break. If he's like his sons, he'll take his time." Both of them draw this out. I like to get information and be done with it. I'm not here for pleasure, just information.

Mr. Segreto doesn't waste time with taunts. He grabs the first tool that speaks to him before going up to the man. Winding back his arm, the man gives us all the information. When we are sure he is finished, he puts a bullet in his head before calling for clean-up.

***

After a quick shower, I go in search of Tony. I'm sure his father is going to tell him that he was shot because of me. I should just pack my stuff and disappear, but I can't. I'm too far gone. As much as it makes sense to let Tony live his life without worrying about me, I can't lose him. This is the first time

I've felt like I have a family.

Thankfully, he is right where I left him. There is some movie on, but he's asleep. I find the doctor in a living room. "Hi Doc. Can you give me an update on Tony?"

He keeps flipping through the channels. "He'll be fine once he rests for a few days. I'd say two or three days. I'm just here to make sure he actually rests and isn't stressed. No need to worry."

Well, if he is going to be safe and doesn't need stress. It's time. I leave without another word. I pack up my bag and sneak out of the house. Tony gave me a spare key to his car so I don't have to steal one since I haven't seen my car. I do steal one of his shirts so I can actually sleep.

It's easier to slip out of the house than I thought it would be. The drive to my old apartment is calm with no following vehicles.

My apartment is exactly how I left it. I haven't been here in a while especially since Matteo picked some of my stuff up before bringing it to Tony's place. I only stayed at a hotel for when they followed me. I needed to know who put the hit on me before I came back.

***

Sleeping in Tony's shirt was the only way I was able to get any rest. I got maybe three hours. It's hard when nobody is watching your back, but nobody knows I'm here. I just need to figure out how to get off the Russians radar.

I also need to finish the work I agreed to do for the family businesses. Keep an eye on Matteo. Get food since nothing is edible in here. I get dressed and make a list for food.

I open my door to Matteo and Mr. Segreto. I was hoping I'd have a full day. In peace, but that's not going to happen. "Get your things." Mr. Segreto announces. I get that he is used to giving orders which are not questioned, but that's not his choice.

"No. This is for the best. I have things to do, so if you don't mind." I try to move between them, but they are basically walls.

Alex always told me how reasonable Matteo was and how level-headed, but he's the one who throws me over his shoulder and carries me to their car. Now there are three other vehicles. I should make a scene, but that will just let the Russians know I'm with them.

I figured I'd be thrown in the backseat and could jump out of the car at the first stop. They seem to have figured that out as well because I'm in the middle. "We will talk when we get back to the house." The ride to his house is deadly quiet. The driver and passenger keep checking the back seat. It is clear they don't trust me and I'm not going to be able to make another run. I need them to let me go.

"It would be safer for all of you if you just drop me off somewhere." Maybe I can convince them without taking me all the way back. "I don't want Tony thinking it was because of him when it was actually *for* him."

"No. You are dealing with Tony. Because he's been losing his mind since he woke up and couldn't find you. When he found Mario, he was told you were sleeping. Apparently, Tony wants Mario's head." Matteo glares at me while speaking.

Well, if Mario is in danger, I have to go back. It isn't his fault that I tricked him. He wasn't there. I made sure he wasn't even on the property when I left. I don't argue. There's no point; plus, I see the house. Someone is going to have to go back to my apartment since I wasn't allowed to grab the stuff I took. I'm also starving so hopefully we can meet and argue in the kitchen.

I'm escorted into the house with the two men flanking me and an entire car full of soldiers who stay outside. I think everyone is going to hear this discussion, but there is no time.

***

Tony is standing at the open door. I stroll right pass him and go to the kitchen. If I'm starting off the day fighting, I'm going to need coffee and food.

"What were you thinking?! I've been worried sick. Did you want me to not heal? Doc said he told you I couldn't be stressed!" He's pacing, but he does look paler.

"Sit." When he doesn't move, I grab his arm and drag him to the chair. "Stressed. Like knowing you were shot because the Russians want me dead? Maybe, I left so you were safe. Maybe, you are in more danger the closer I am to you. Maybe, you should have thought why I would leave and not that I am your possession and you can take me from my home. Did you consider any of that? Or did you just go off the rails?"

I watch all the men move their hands to their weapons, but I take the gun Mr. Segreto gave me and place it on the table. I don't need to risk them shooting each other. Although, I'm sure doc is still around.

All wind is out of his sails now. "Why would I care if I got shot because of you? I wouldn't be able to live with myself if you got shot instead of me. What if you were killed?"

At least we are on the same page here. Who is going to be more stubborn? "You are in this family. Getting shot isn't too shocking, so you definitely don't need me adding to your risk. Also, I care that you were shot! Why do you think I left? Why do you think I handled both of the men involved? Yes, others found them, but I wasn't going to not get myself involved."

The more I think about it, I don't think we should have an audience for this entire conversation. It might turn too personal. I go over next to him and whisper. "Let's finish this alone."

He looks from me to the growing audience before nodding. I let him led us to the bedroom I set him up in. When we get to the door, I stop. "Mario, please wait with the others. I'm not going to leave I promise. I left when you weren't on duty for a reason."

He looks over my head before turning and heading back. I close and lock the door. "Should I be worried? You've never locked a door."

I smirk because he is actually worried. "I don't want to be interrupted. A locked door will delay someone trying to barge in." He doesn't know the things I have planned. I hope he can handle it, but I have a feeling he will ignore all the signs saying he can't handle it.

"First, thank you for suggesting a private conversation. The men in the family are the biggest gossips." He smiles but it doesn't last. With an unsteady voice, "Why would you think the best choice was to leave without telling me?"

For the first time since I made the decision to leave, I actually feel guilty. "You shouldn't have the burden of keeping me safe. I figured you would try to talk me out of leaving or do something that would put you at more risk. Without your knowledge, I hoped you would just move on and forget about me. That way, nobody could use me against you. You'd be free."

"Did you forget that I love you, mostriciattola? You leaving without saying a word wasn't going to snap my feelings for you. When I woke up and couldn't find you, I was more worried than I have ever been. Even more so when Matteo, dad, and Mario had no clue you had even left. I don't want to feel that dread again." He pushes my chin up so we're looking at each other. "Can you please promise me that whatever you think is the best option, you talk to me first? Don't just act."

"I promise." I don't think that was the right thing to promise, but I need to tell him the truth.

"What's the real reason you left?" How does a man who has known me for less than a year read me better than anyone I've known?

"I figured that leaving might stop me from continuing to fall in love with you. I finally get what Alex meant when he said I'll know when my person comes into my life if I let them. I hate that you have so much power over me. I hate that if we are together, because of who your family is, you'll want to keep things from me. I don't want to not know. I don't want to be told to sit still and look pretty. I want to be involved. I need to keep you safe and I can't if I'm kept in the dark. But more so, I knew my being with you would cause you to be in harms way."

I kept my eyes closed so I didn't have to see his reaction. When he doesn't respond, I slowly open them. He looks paler? I should have gotten a full run down on his condition, medications, things to avoid, but I didn't. My heart had risked too much already. I push him back so he's sitting on the edge of the bed. I kneel down to check his wound, which is fine.

"What's wrong?" I pull out my phone to get the doc here when he pulls me to him.

"Nothing, except I need this and I don't know what I can do." He kisses me. Not one of those soft, loving ones he loves in the morning. No, this is a claiming. He's marking me as his. I kiss him back with the same vigor. If I'm his, he's mine. I don't care that there is a room full of men down the hall. I don't care that this is his father's house, roof. We both need this.

He tugs at my shirt and I break the kiss only to remove it. He took that opportunity to remove his. Clothes are flying. Nothing can get off quick enough. I guide him further onto the bed. Usually, he likes to take control, but with him still healing, I take the chance. I get his back against the headboard before kissing my way down his body. How was I going to be able to walk away from this?

When I reach his hard length, I slide my fist up and down while twirling my tongue around his tip. All at once, his body tightens and loosens in the right spots. I feel the tension melt away.

I focus all my attention on his tip, which is already beading. I love how much he enjoys this, but I need more. I can't push him too far since I don't want to hurt him. Doc said two to three days, we can wait for the perfect joining when he's healed.

Except, he fists my hair. I look up at him without breaking my ministrations. "I need you. Now." He grunts.

I keep my hands working. "Not until you are one hundred percent. Doc said two to three days. You can hold on. I'll make it worth the wait." I smile before taking him entirely. I feel him close, so I increase my speed and pressure. With my hands freed up, I reach around and play with his balls. Nothing like that to push him over. I swallow all of him before looking back up at him.

Chapter 20

Tony

"I need you to come up here. Sit on my face. I'm having dessert. There is no way I can wait that long to have your taste on my tongue." I demand, she looks unsure. I do the one thing I know will help. I pull her up my body as I slide onto my back.

She still looks uncertain, but that all changes as I run my tongue up her slit. That stops her argument. I hear her moan as I lightly suck on her clit. She needs to loosen up, so I take my time. I have nothing better to do than make sure she never leaves me again.

My wound is on my left so I part her lips with my fingers before diving in. after a few moments focusing on her entrance, she starts to relax. I push my fingers in while my lips cover her clit. I hum my agreement as she pushes her pussy onto my face. Exactly, she does some of the work, I help out. No stitches tear. Doc doesn't have to know. Then, I can be cleared by tomorrow night, hopefully, and have my way with her entire body.

I slowly plunge my fingers deep inside while focusing my mouth elsewhere. She's close, and even though I want this to last and draw it out, I'm already tiring. I need a nap from all that stress. Plus, the orgasm she gave me. I increase the speed of my fingers, easily finding the spot deep inside before humming around her clit.

Her legs tighten around my head as I feel her spasm around my fingers. I drink it all in. This is too good to let go to waste. When I feel her legs relax and her muscle stop, I pull back. "Wanna take a shower then a nap?" I ask.

She nods and leads me to the shower. Maybe showering together isn't a good idea. I've been picturing her against the wall as I drive into her. Her legs wrapped around my waist; her hands tangled in my hair. At least we know each other's feelings because I'm hard again.

***

She falls asleep next to me, but not on me. When she arrived at the house, I knew she didn't sleep. I should be sleeping as well, but there is one person I need to talk to.

Walking into the living room, it seems most of the men are gone. "Mario. Can you please wait outside the bedroom in case she wakes up? I just need a few minutes with my dad." There is only one room that is soundproof that isn't hidden. "Can we talk in your office?"

My dad and I walk to his office in silence. For the first time, I don't think he knows what we need to talk about. But if Dani needs to be let in, I need to know that is doable before I try to keep her. I shut the door behind me. No need to lock it since anyone that walks through the door without knocking will be killed.

Steeling myself for his reaction that will not be pretty, I start. "Daniella gave me a condition to continue our relationship. She doesn't want to be kept in the dark and I don't want to have to lie to her. I know it's not smart to let her know everything, but you and Matteo need to know she will be aware. She's not some wallflower I can keep in the dark. If I don't tell her, she'll find it out herself which will be worse for all of us."

Don't play poker with my dad. I thought I'd know what I was expecting to come out, but it wasn't this. "And this is news how?" He hasn't reacted at all since I came in. "I always knew you would need a partner that was involved. Why do you think I allowed her to come to the warehouses? I also haven't been hiding what we are doing when she is around."

"So, you are fine with her staying involved? Will Matteo be fine with this when you retire?" Hopefully, that isn't going to happen anytime soon, but I need to be aware if it's going to be a problem later.

My dad doesn't answer, but he does start tapping his desk. "Enter." His response to the knocking at the door. Matteo strolls in. He must have gotten a text.

"When you take over, will you change who Tony is allowed to share information with that I have already approved?" Well, that's cryptic.

"You mean will I be ok with Daniella knowing what Tony is doing and keeping her involved in the family?" Not that cryptic, I guess. My dad nods once. "Yeah. I don't have any issues with that. Hopefully, that won't be my decision for a while."

"Thanks, you can head back out if you'd like." More of dismissal than we ever get, but he lingers.

He never looks uncertain, but he is. This only makes me worry. "Are you planning to propose?"

We've discussed a lot in this office, but it's never been this quiet. My eyes are on his, but my dad is watching me. "Not today, but eventually, I'd like to." We don't have these talks.

He nods. "Alex left me his mother's ring for me to give to the person planning to propose to her. When you are ready, I'll give you the ring."

With that news, we break from the meeting. I go back to the bedroom and get some rest now that I have my own answers. When I get to the door, Mario isn't there. I burst through the door to find both of them. Nobody is bleeding or yelling, so I'm not sure why Mario felt the need to enter.

I guess my thoughts are on my face. "I was just apologizing to Mario for getting him in trouble even though he had nothing to do with it. I also made sure he was aware that he will not receive any punishment for my actions."

I look over at him who is still looking uncertain that he should believe her. "You will remain her shadow for as long as you would like to.

You are the only one I trust with her, which is why she probably waited until you weren't on before leaving."

Daniella blushes, but Mario just nods before stepping out. "Why didn't you sleep after you suggested the nap?" Ah, her fire is back. I thought she might try to ice me out but after our reunion, I'm glad we are back to an agreement.

I kiss her before pulling her back to bed. "I wanted to talk to my dad. I was concerned about your condition, but he and my brother agreed that it would be fine. My dad apparently knew that would be a condition to my partner. Plus, he's let you in on more details than some of the men."

***

We spent the last two days watching movies. She hasn't left my side. Making sure I have everything I need. Yelling at anyone who tries to get in between us. She sent Mario to her place to get the items she took home. It's nice to see the two of them getting along. Mario has been lingering everywhere we are.

Doc cleared me after breakfast. Let's just say waiting for your dad to leave his house as an adult hits a little differently. The tension between Dani and me has been growing since she came back.

We had lunch together, but she left quickly after to leave me with dad and Matteo. I don't know how to kick anyone out of a house that I don't own. "Daniella and I are going to go back to my place since I'm all cleared."

"No." Well, that's not helpful. "You will stay here until we figure out why the Russians put a hit on her. Also, Mario will be with her at all times. No sending him away." I groan as he walks away.

"It's a good thing we both have meetings all night." Thank God for Matteo. My eyes snap to his, which are laughing. It's been too long since I saw him somewhat happy. He still blames himself for Alex. However, something is going on with him.

Now, we just need to make it to tonight without anyone pulling a trigger. Enough guns have been pulled, just no shots fired. Apparently, the gun Dani brought to the meeting with my dad was fake, which explains why he gave her a real one. Not that she needs one.

I need to find Mario and give him the night off before I get some work done so I can focus tonight. Maybe I should take a nap, too. I need one of Dani's lists. Dani is already in her makeshift office working away. I swear this woman is now running most of the companies herself. She also implemented a lot of procedures to make everything more effective. If I wasn't worried, I'd say she's after my job.

Mario is sitting in the library, which seems to be his favorite spot. Probably because it gives him access to hear everything going on in the house and a quick route to Dani. "Mario. You have off tonight. Go home. Do something fun."

He's my right hand. If I give an order, that's not too out there, he goes along without question. "Ah, boss. No can do." I lift my eyebrows. He has never refused an order. "Your dad stopped me before he left to tell me that under no circumstances am I allowed to let either of you leave here. I can't do that if I'm not here."

Damnit dad. "You will be in bed early tonight. On the opposite wing from our room. I don't care if you hear screaming. The only thing that should cause you to break down our door is gunshots. Understood?"

A shit-eating grin appears on his face. I guess everyone is going to know my plans tonight. "Gunshots. Got it." He nods before returning to his book.

***

After a filling dinner with Mario, he excuses himself to bed. "Is he feeling alright? Do you think we should have doc look him over?"

I know Dani has grown fond of him, but I think it's her observation skills that need to relax. "He's fine. Just following orders." I planned on making a scene at dinner like one of her favorite books, but I couldn't with Mario observing. "Done?"

She nods and takes some of the plates. We've falling into a rhythm. She washes the dishes while I'll put leftovers into containers. It makes easy and quick work. Plus, no more broken plates like the first night she cleaned and told us to get helping.

As soon as the water is off, I throw her over my shoulder. I'm done being gentle and patient. She's mine and I'm going to make sure the neighbors know it. Not that my dad has any neighbors. She feels this too because she isn't trying to get away.

As soon as I enter our room, I close and door and pin her to it. I take her lips in a savage kiss. Nothing will be left tonight. She opens immediately, wrapping her legs around my waist to pull me closer. Her hands end up in my hair. My hands knead her ass as I keep her lips at my height.

I slowly set her down on her feet without breaking the kiss, so I can get clothes off. I know I want to explore and take it slow, but first, it needs to be hard and fast. We have all night, but I'm not going to last if I go slow.

She seems to be following my train of thought. She breaks the kiss and our shirts join the rest of our clothes. I always felt she would submit in the bedroom, but I love that she takes control some. She pushes my chest so I'm walking backwards to the bed. As soon as my legs hit it, I sit.

When she climbs on my lap and straddles me, I know this will be just one of many orgasms I wring out of her. Without missing a beat, I press my tip into her softness. I thought she might still, but this is a first for us, she needs to go at her own pace before I slam into her.

I return to kissing her, but I leave her lips. I take one breast in my mouth and the other in my hand. My other hand is on her hip, encouraging her to take what she needs. She needs to start moving or this is going to get ugly.

As soon as my breathe touches her skin, she starts moving. I flick her nipple at the same time she sinks all the way onto me and she moans. I guess she didn't need to warm up. All day has been a warm up though.

We fall into a pattern as she grinds against me. Everything is greedy. Hands, mouths, sounds. In record time, I'm pulsing inside her with her close behind. She drains me of every drop possible as she comes down from hers.

I pull out of her and twist so she's on her back. I start crawling up her body when I realize we forgot something. A condom. I'm clean, I bet she is too. But we don't need babies right now. I want to get to know her and have her all to myself.

"I'm covered." She is the only person that can read me so well.

I smile as I drop my face between her thighs. The last time we did this, she had control. This time, she's not going to get any say. I kiss up her legs as I push them back. With her legs up, so she can't use those legs against me, I take my first long languid lick up her slit. She's so wet from the first orgasm that I don't need any teasing.

I press my tongue as far in as possible before licking around. I repeat a few times to get her writhing. When she groans in frustration, I move to her clit. Sucking and nipping, I play. I insert two fingers right away and focus my mouth elsewhere. She wastes no time coming. I drink her all in. This is too good to let go to waste.

Getting that orgasm gave my dick time to recover and get ready to go back in. I already have her in position, so I place a pillow under her ass and thrust in. Hard. The sound of my name on her lips almost has me coming already. I set a slow, punishing past. Pulling out to just the tip before thrusting all the way back in.

"Faster." I smirk at her demand and go even slower. Her groan nearly undoes me. She starts meeting my thrusts to make them what she wants. I lean down over her to get a better look when she takes my mouth in a soft kiss.

I almost pull all the way out, but the change in tempo makes me weak. She wraps her legs around me and flips me onto my back with her on top. As soon as my back hits the bed, she's sliding all the way down. The sight of her breasts bouncing has me bucking hard into her. She rides me out as her orgasm slowly fades having started first.

Chapter 21

Daniella

As soon as the third orgasm ends, I'm pulled on top of Tony. No words need to be spoken, but slowly our breathing and hearts return to normal. Before I know it, Tony's hand is soothing my hair and I'm drifting off to the beat of his heart.

Thankfully, we both slept the entire night, but now that I'm rested, I'm ready for the next round. I don't know if his father ever returned last night or if Mario is still in the house. I do know the bathroom should be private enough. I roll onto Tony before kissing his lips with a soft promise. I'm off him as quickly as I got on.

"Where are you going?" Sleep still muffles his voice.

I peel off his shirt that I threw on in the middle of the night. I'm still not comfortable sleeping completely naked. If there is a fire, I don't want to have to either grab clothes first or talk to someone without clothes on. "I'm going to take a shower and I could use some help with my back." I look over my shoulder before promptly walking into the wall.

Miss judged that distance. Oh, that's going to bruise. "Shit." That got him out of bed. "Let me see." I turn around and he strokes the side of my head. "Anything else besides your head?" I shake my head and instantly regret it. "Shower and pleasure first. I'll have doc check you for a concussion after breakfast."

I don't know much, but doc better be on payroll or retainer or something. That man should have a room here as well.

I wanted to make this about him, but as soon as the water is warm, he is pushing into me as he shampoos my hair at the same time. I can't focus on all the sensations. The tightness and fullness as he plunges into me. The feel of his lips against my ear and neck. His hands in my hair to clean. The worst part, my back is against his front. I can't touch him or get any traction. I'm completely at his will.

He pulls out when he finishes my hair. "My turn." He pushes back in, but letting me face him. I sit him on the bench and do the same process with him. Shampoo, rinse, condition, rinse. But this time, I don't slide out. I lather his chest and arms and face, but I wait until we both come before rinsing. I then finish washing the rest of his body. Before cleaning and rinsing myself.

He wrapped me in a warm towel as soon as I stepped out of the shower, which I threw off a tad aggressively. I don't get why dry towels are warm. I grab a room temperature towel and dry off. He placed my towel back in a box. "Was it not warm enough?" He's confused. I guess growing up like he did, hot towels were normal.

"Warm towels feel damp. This towel felt dry when I started unlike the one you wrapped around me. Plus, I'll overheat. It's not like we didn't just take a hot shower." His skin is still red from the water. "What are your plans for today?"

I feel his gaze track my body while saying. "So much." Before he picks me up and carries me back to bed. He pulled the towel off, but his eyes freeze. "Did I hurt you?"

I follow his eyes to my waist. I guess I should have told him about the easily bruising thing. "You'll hurt my feelings if you hold back. They will heal." I pull his head down and make him forget about the bruises.

***

Matteo drug me into the office for a few meetings this morning. I didn't want to leave Tony at the house, but space might be a good idea. He's been nearly insatiable the last few nights. Once he got that all clear, he's been testing his limits. Not that I mind.

We just finished our second meeting and everyone has finally cleared out of the conference room. Most of these meetings could be an email. However, you can't send an angry stare and threaten people with a look in an email, so in person meetings it is. If I'm going to be in here, I'd like to get some of my actual work done.

I'm putting my stuff into a pile to take to my office. "Leave it." I give Matteo my best *what the fuck* look I can muster. Sleeping with Tony at night hasn't left much time for, well, actual sleeping. "We have a lunch meeting and then another back in here, so no reason to put everything away to take it back out." He stands up and opens the door before dramatically holding it open for me.

One thing I never noticed before is how empty the office gets at lunch. Some go home; others out; rarely does anyone pack a lunch and eat at their desk. I typically don't see that when I'm in different offices. It's nice though. Everyone is actually treated like a person. Not a robot.

"I had lunch brought in. Mario got it so I know it is something you will actually eat." I see Mario sitting in my office on the couch with the largest sandwich possible. How it fits on the bagel? No idea. Plus, a bag of chips. If I hadn't been around him so much, it would look weird.

The first time he got me a sandwich from his mom's place, I requested he call her right away so I could tell her how amazing it was. I rush into his office and plop down before finding my sandwich. Screw manners. This is too good to wait for. "Thanks for lunch." I say around my second bite.

I'm about halfway finished when I realize he hasn't taken a single bite. I'm not a fast eater, but these are too good. Why did I look up? "What's wrong?" When he doesn't answer, I put my sandwich on my plate. "Stop pacing. You have my complete attention."

He pours a glass of scotch and downs it before refilling it. "I don't know what to do." That's it. He goes for a third shot, but if he's anything like his brother, that won't help. I grab the bottle before he can pour another. "What would Alex want me to do with him gone? He was supposed to be my person."

"How long have you been sitting on this?" He won't meet my eyes which hasn't happened means since I came back into his life. "What do you think he'd want more than anything in the world? Except to be here with you." I add that on when he goes to answer immediately.

We both know he didn't leave by his choice. "Part of me thinks he would want me to move on. Remember him, but find someone to love. Nobody to replace him, but someone who makes me smile. That's what I told him to do if something happened to me. But I'm selfish. I want him. It took long enough to find him. I didn't get him for long."

"Why are you asking me? You already know what he needs you to do." I read the letter he left. After I saw the ring box, I knew what I would find inside.

"Because you're his sister. You know him. Better than I did. Better than anyone. He always said how you helped him through your parents' deaths. Can't you help me through this?"

If only it were that easy. "Grief doesn't get fixed like that. I helped him because he knew what he needed out of me. He knew I'd get revenge and deal with any issues. He said I helped him, but he allowed me to do what I needed to do to help him. He didn't sleep until the person responsible wasn't breathing. I never told him what happened, but he finally slept that night."

I looked over at him and he was finally sitting down. "When was the last time you slept?" I doubt he's gotten any by the bags under his eyes.

"Last night." The answer is automatic.

"Try again. This time, don't lie."

"I can't sleep without him. I've tried everything. Doc's given me stuff, which hasn't worked. I tried drinking, exercising, none of it has even made a dent."

I don't want to do this, but Tony can last one night. "Stay at your dad's tonight. I have something that might work." I don't tell him what, but I'm going to need to talk to Mario before our next meeting. "Eat your sandwich. I'll thank Mario."

I leave, with my sandwich. After the first day, Mario knows not to
144

jump up when I walk in. I'm not the queen. I also spook easily, so. "Thanks for the food. Tell Ma it's amazing as always." He nods and pulls out his phone. "I also need a favor."

I wait until he sends the text before I close the door. Matteo doesn't need to know my plans, but I also don't want to 'out' him to anyone. "Can you go to my brother's place and grab a few things?"

"You have a brother?" We haven't had any heart to hearts yet. I'm just his assignment, a fun one, but still work. Why get to know me?

"I did. He was friends with Matteo." That much is true. Really, really good friends, but friendship was the base for their love. "If I give you a list and an address, do you think it is possible?" I know he is supposed to stay with me, but I'm not going to leave without him. "I promise to stay with Matteo in this office building until you return."

I hold my breath while he weighs the options. "Fine. But. Not a lot of stuff and I have to be gone from here for less than an hour."

"I can work with that." I quickly jot down a few necessities. Some shirts, his pillow, and my favorite stuffy of his. With the list, a key, and the address, I send Mario on his way and return to the dreaded conference room.

"Has anyone ever been killed in this room? Death by boredom?" I'm asking myself out loud when someone chuckles. Nobody is supposed to be in here. "My apologies. I didn't realize another meeting was scheduled." I turn to leave when I hear someone get out of their chair.

"That's not normal. Typically, nobody jokes about murder in these offices." I'm about to scream when Matteo walks in.

"Ah, Daniella, I had the dates wrong. We are meeting tomorrow after lunch." He shoots me a look I've never seen before from him, but many times from his dad.

"Not a problem. I have a lot of other things to accomplish before that meeting anyway. Let me grab these items so you all can enjoy your meeting." I grab the giant pile of items and the bag I left. As soon as I get to the office I was set up in, I realize someone has been through all my stuff. At least the computer is still on my desk. Locked.

***

When Mario texts that he made it back, I respond and meet him there. The drive to the house is weird. I like Mario, don't get me wrong, but how do I explain what just happened.

I carry the duffle of stuff into the house after fighting Mario about it. He at least leads me to Tony right away before disappearing. I've found him in the library mostly. Usually has a book on him. "Hey, can you take me to your brother's room?" Tony's eyebrows are hidden by his hair now. "Without making a scene?"

He stands and tries to grab the bag, but fails. They need better grips honestly. I'm not even holding it that firmly. I held another part of him firmer less than 24 hours ago. The memory of him coming that quickly with my hands wrapped around him has me smirking. I never would have imagined making a man unravel so much and as easily as I can with him would make me feel giddy.

"What's that look for?" I hate that he is able to tell my thoughts without even looking at me.

"If you behave, I'll show you later. If not, I'll tell you." The handcuffs have not come into play after he broke the headboard. The look on his face tells me they will tonight though. Too bad, no funny business tonight. "Your brother is spending the night here."

"He hasn't slept since you came back, has he?" One thing I love about Tony is his love for Matteo.

I shake my head. I need Tony to know enough to not cause issues, but not too much that he involves himself. It was hard for Matteo to tell me how difficult it's been. And I'm living through it too. It's a weird relationship we have, but I'm glad he trusts me to tell me. "Not since he last saw Alex. So, I'm going to set up his room to make it impossible not to."

The room is the exact same as Tony's bedroom. Just neater. I put the pillow on his bed and place the shirts everywhere. Now the big move. Stuffy needs the best place possible. "What side does he sleep on?"

I'm looking at the bed, but it's not like Matteo spends every night here. "People don't have sides. They sleep on their bed." Nope. Not even close. Everyone has a favored side. Well, Alex liked the right, so I guess Matteo was given the left. I set Stuffy up and step back. This should do the trick.

I grab Tony's arm and we leave before he can ask questions or start rearranging.

Matteo is walking down the hall as we are leaving. I push Tony the other direction. Surely there is another set of stairs in this house for him to get back. "What are you doing over here?"

I open his door and wait for him to go inside first. "If you are up for it, maybe we can have his favorite take out for dinner and watch one of the movies I'm sure he forced you to watch. I have a feeling it might help so you can get a good night's sleep."

"How did you get it to smell like him?" The voice is so small that I almost don't hear him. He picks up a shirt before grabbing the stuffy. "What was his obsession with foxes about?"

I remember the day he brought that home. "He won it at the carnival. It was the dime toss and he got a quarter completely covering the dot, but since it was a quarter, he got the smaller prize, which is still decent sized."

"Maybe tomorrow we can do that stuff. I think I'd like to be left alone." I nod and close his door before I hear his first sob.

Chapter 22

Tony

Walking into our bedroom, I follow the sniffles. Dani is curled into a ball on the bed. I always forget how small she is. I quickly change into pajamas and climb in beside her. I pull her onto my lap and let her get it out.

It could have been a few minutes or an hour, but with a soaked shirt and red eyes, the tears stop. "You wanna talk about it?"

She sniffs and leans against me. "I spoke with Matteo and I set up a room with Alex's stuff to help him sleep." I was there when she set everything up, so why is she telling me this?

"That made you upset?"

"I just miss him and seeing how much pain Matteo is in, it hurts. I got to bury him, but he didn't get that closure. I know how much Alex loved him, but he never got to live with him. They both have regrets and I don't want any."

"What do you feel you will regret?" I lean back and take her face in my hand. "You can talk to me. I'm not going to get up and leave."

Fresh tears in her eyes. "I don't want to miss out on love and living life. I've been so focused on revenge and protecting Alex. I don't know what I want anymore. I've fallen too hard too fast. What if this doesn't last?"

"I'm not going anywhere." I squeeze her and keep her close.

"When you got shot, I couldn't think straight. Your father tried to stop me from tracking down the person and he failed. I defied your father because I felt too much. I couldn't sit and watch you in pain without being able to do anything. The only thing I could do was hurt them. You might not want to go anywhere, but that isn't your choice. What about the hit? Someone wants to take me from you."

"Shhh, it's going to be alright. I have plans in motion to figure out how to get rid of your hit. Yes, I was shot, but you were there with me when it mattered. I get not sitting by and doing nothing. I'd rather you take out your anger on the guy that shot me. I would never expect you to stop being passionate and wanting to hurt someone who hurt someone you care for."

I lay down and let her fall asleep on me after she soaks my shirt again with her tears.

***

It's been too long since I've been in the office. I don't mind working from home, but leaving the work in the office is always nice. It's uncommon for all of us to be here at the same time, but if we are going to confront Hal, we need to have each other's backs.

"Is Fred also coming or is it just the four of us?" Since I've been shot, dad and Matteo have kept me out of everything to give me time to recover. It's not like I haven't been working more since then. Sleep has been better with Dani next to me. After we exhaust each other with our bodies, we typically pass out. But I wake up refreshed. Also, no commute.

They are both staring at me. "Why would we bring Fred?" "Have you not listened to a thing we said the entire ride here?"

Great, this is back. "So, we can verify he wasn't involved. Also, we are going to need to divide Hal's work between the three of us unless you have another plan. It makes sense bringing him in now. You two didn't speak the entire ride! I was stuck in the back like a toddler."

They don't answer me as the door opens and Hal walks in. I guess we aren't going with a plan. "What's the meeting for?" He will never accept Matteo as the head so it might be a good thing he is not going to be around when he takes over.

My dad is seated behind his desk with Matteo directly over his shoulder. Hal sits across from my dad, but I stay by the door. His mistake. "Something has been brought to my attention. Do you want to share something with me?"

"What are you talking about? You are always kept in the loop with me." My dad sighs. He knew Hal wasn't going to outright admit anything, but this is going to get bad.

"I'm always kept in the loop? Alright, how much money have you stolen from me?"

I see Hal reach behind him. "No." I grab his hands. He might be older and respected, but the fact that he's been lying and stealing throws all that out. I pull his gun out and take it from him. "Tell the truth or we will move this meeting to a warehouse." He knows how ruthless I get in the warehouse and my dad will gladly let me have my way.

"Fine. It was just a little. Your father set it up and I kept it operating." Half the truth is better than none.

"Just a little. Why have I heard it was more than a few hundred grand in the last year?" My dad is pissed. Lying to him once is stupid. The second time is a death sentence. We already knew he wasn't walking out though. "If you have been doing this since my father, that would be how many decades?"

"Kill me. I won't talk." My dad looks over Hal's shoulder and looks at me. As much as dad wants to kill him, he prefers to keep his hands clean. I walk up and snap his neck. No reason to need a clean-up crew.

"Who is going to cover Hal's work?" I ask. I text one of my guys who is downstairs to take care of his body.

The two of them share a look. "How serious are you about Daniella? When are you planning to propose?" Change of topic much.

How do I answer that? "Why does that matter?" Why do they keep
150

asking about marriage?

"I want her to take over for Hal. She'll be able to get our legit businesses more profitable than our other businesses." My dad announces. There's no option to deny.

"You want her to be involved in the businesses?" This is ridiculous. We don't let our women get involved. We talked but I still didn't believe she'd be actively involved.

Matteo speaks up. "We know she won't just sit by and not be kept in the loop. She is smart enough to know how to deal with our business, extremely trustworthy, and she has done enough things for the family already."

"It's her choice." As soon as the words are out of my mouth, I turn to leave. My dad is going to have to ask her. I'm staying out of this.

***

I left the meeting with my dad and brother to go to another meeting. Walking into the Russian's office, I've only been here a few times, but all the men know who I am.

"Ah, Tony. Thanks for coming here. How are you doing?" Dmitri asks.

I nod to him. "Thanks for having me. I'm doing well. As I said over the phone, I just have one question and I'll leave you to enjoy the night." He signals me to continue on. "There is a hit on a lady, Daniella. I want to know two things. Who put the hit on her and why?"

He passes me a glass of vodka. The damn Russians and their vodka. "Why do you care?"

"Well, it's not common for a female to have a hundred thousand hit on them. I haven't found something that gives a good reason for that." I try to look relaxed. We've become friendly enough since my dad let me take over this relationship. Our fathers used to be at each other's throats. After the first meeting, we decided to try to get along instead of trying to constantly kill one another.

"You must not have heard that she can torture anyone with no mercy. Also, her brother stuck his nose in our business which led to his death. We don't know what he told her, so we want her taken care of."

So, Alex was killed by the Russians. "Does she know anything? Our families typically leave the women out of everything."

He finishes his glass and refills it, twice. "It's not my thoughts. I want to let it go. She hasn't done anything enough to warrant her death. That's my boss's decision."

"You and me don't agree with it. Maybe we should do something to remove the threat from her. Do you think that is possible?" I have a feeling he doesn't want this on his conscious.

He refills my glass. "If you want to talk to my father. I've tried."

"What if I find her and see if she knows anything, then bring the information to you and we can talk with your father?" I need to get rid of this hit without showing my cards.

"Deal. I'll speak to my father before bringing you back."

Without another word, we part ways. The drive to my dad's is tense. My men don't know why I had to meet with Dmitri. They just knew I had to go alone and they needed to handle everything else. There's too much I need to discuss with Dani. First, dad wants her to join the family business. Now, I need to know what she knows about the Russians.

Walking into the house, I check our bedroom and she is out cold. I tuck her in and head back downstairs. Matteo is sitting there. "Can't sleep?"

He shakes his head and changes the channel. "You're going to marry her, aren't you?"

I really don't want to deal with this. "I hope so." I grab us drinks and go sit next to him. "Is that a problem with you?"

He downs the drink. "She's perfect for you. We want you to be happy, but she's something else. When I first met her with Alex, I knew you two would become thick as thieves. I just expected it to be my wedding you fell for her at. I'm happy that she came into your life."

That was one of our deals growing up. We can't be pissed if one of us finds our person and the other doesn't. Neither of us expected him to find his and lose him though.

"The Russians want her dead. They killed Alex." His head slowly shifts to me. The TV show forgotten. "I met with Dmitri after our meeting. He explained Alex found out something and had to be killed for it. He's the reason Dmitri's father took out the hit on Dani. I have to find out what she knows and then meet with them again to get the hit removed."

"Oh man. Can't we just have a nice night?" He gets up and leaves the room. With that bomb, he's going to need some time.

***

I left a note on the vanity for Dani since I got back later than I expected. After last night I realized I never took her on a date. After clearing the idea with dad and security, I called and made reservations at a restaurant. A dress is being delivered later today for Dani to change into.

I'm waiting in the foyer waiting for her to come downstairs. Mario is in the library already since he'll be escorting us. "Mario, get the car ready. I'm going up to get her."

I don't wait for a response before taking the stairs two at a time. Forgetting to knock, I barge into our bedroom. I get an eyeful of her back. She's also twisting and looking into the mirror at the same time. "Thank God. Can you zip me up?" I walk up to help her. "Usually, I can do it myself, but this zipper is smaller than the ones I'm used to."

As soon as the zipper reaches the top, she grabs my hand and leads us downstairs. "Why didn't you come to the foyer? I would have helped you instead of pacing."

"You wanted me to leave our bedroom without my dress secured so a soldier could find me half naked with a dress in a chokehold?"

When she puts it like that, her choice makes sense. "No. You did the right thing. Are you ready?" She nods, but I see her smirk. This is going to be a great night.

The ride to the restaurant is quiet. Some small talk, but nothing more.

153

We are going to have all night to talk. We get seated at the table I reserved with the one guard watching the back and Mario at the bar near the entrance. "Thank you for the dress."

"You look lovely in it. I wanted to do something special since everything has been a tad crazy." If tonight goes how I think it will, I'm going to need the ring from Matteo.

She snorts without even looking away from the menu. We order when the waitress comes before slipping back into small talk. This feels like the weirdest date. I've already fucked her multiple times. Why do I want to know what her favorite color is?

"Ok, I have a very important question. Where do you want to live?" I realize I've taken her from a hotel to my penthouse to my dad's house. We are going to need a place of our own. I wouldn't mind having her move into the penthouse, but I think we should go bigger if we are going to have kids.

She takes a sip of water while my scotch sits almost completely empty. "I want a place with a yard. Maybe some space between neighbors. What about you? What drew you to the penthouse?"

"I got to be in the middle of everything, which was nice when Matteo or one of the guys would want to go out. Plus, a few of my guys lived there already which made it feel safer." I don't tell her that I made the entire floor below me only my men.

"Do you want to stay there forever?"

I see the answers in her face. She wants to build a home with me. Or that is what I'm hoping I'm seeing. "No. I'd like a yard for the kids and pets, too."

"Kids? How many do you want?" Smooth. Just drop that word.

I never thought about having children before her. Now, I'd love to see a miniature Dani growing up. "As many as you'd like to have. If that is none, I would be fine with just having you."

She opens her mouth to respond, but our food arrives. We eat in comfortable silence.

As we get back into the car. "Thank you for dinner." She looks over and kisses me. I don't tell her that we are not finished with the night. "Where are we going?"

We have pulled up to the Metropolitan Museum. "Well, dinner was part one. This is part two. We sometimes get invited to the Met Gala, so I figured you should see the museum at least once before.

I hold my hand out so she comes out my door. We walk up the iconic steps and start making on our way through all the exhibits. I feel her relax again for the first time from our children talk.

Chapter 23

Daniella

I don't want the date to end, but the museum is closing. Finally. They let us stay an hour later than we were allowed to because of Tony. I felt bad though, so I lied and said I wanted to go home.

"Are you feeling alright? Was it dinner?" He keeps looking at me since we got into the car.

"Just tired. Thank you for tonight." I think everything going on is finally catching up to me. Too much has happened in such a short time span. At least Tony is going to let me sleep tonight since I had us end the date earlier than he wanted to.

We pull into the driveway and it's full of cars. This can't be good, but we didn't receive any calls or texts that I know of. I look at Tony and he shakes his head. "What's going on? Are we supposed to be here?"

"Everything is fine. Yes, we can be here. I'm going to get you into our room and then check in with my dad." I don't like the sound of that. Ever since I said I was tired, my body is finally realizing the truth, so I don't fight him on it.

Once we enter his bedroom, that's now ours, I go to bring him with me to the shower. He stands firm though. I raise my eyebrows. He's not one to turn down anything physical I offer. Something is really going on. "I'll be back as soon as I can. Do not open this door for anyone. The four people that are allowed in here have keys." He kisses my forehead before locking the door on his way out.

***

Ever feel like the new kid even though nothing changed from the day before except a title? Walking into the office with the official title of employee is making everybody act weird. I know I got the job through non-disclosed means, but I have worked my ass off to get where I am.

After failing at getting rid of my office, I quickly close the door as soon as I'm over the threshold. Mario at least only has to drive me now instead of standing guard at my door. The hit is still on me, but since I'm an employee, I'm more protected.

Each time I try to get work done, I hear the whispers of people right outside my door. None of it is nice either. I tried playing music to block them, but nothing is helping. I'm tempted to start drinking. If I'm drunk, I won't care, but that would cause more issues.

This was a bad idea. I shouldn't work for the family business. I should resign and continue working as a consultant. That might hurt Mr. Segreto's feelings though. He'd take it as a personal slight even though it's just too much.

I start thinking about all the changes that happened since Alex died and it's too much. He should be here with me to make sure I'm on track and not losing my mind. I feel the panic start. It's too hot in here, so I start stripping. My door's closed so nobody will just walk in on me. The clothes off didn't help. I go into the connected bathroom and run some water over my wrists. Great. Making it worse. Screw it. I hope in the shower. Why is there a shower in my office? No clue, but maybe it'll help.

I don't know how long I'm standing in there, but the water finally starts to feel cold on my skin. Stepping out of the shower, shivering, I look for a towel. Probably should have found one first. That thought throws me back into the spiral.

157

I hop back in the shower after texting Matteo about the towels. I hear the ding, but it doesn't register. The phone keeps dinging, so I turn the noise off. Should I have looked at it first, yes, but logical brain isn't working.

I try exiting the shower again only to slip when I hear banging on the office door. Oops. I locked it and I'm not opening it naked. I freeze on the floor of the shower.

Mr. Segreto, Matteo, and Mario are staring at me from the open bathroom door. I should be more concerned about being naked, but my eyes are locked on the towel Matteo is holding. "Why was your door locked?" This comes from Mr. Segreto who turned around as soon as he realized I was naked.

"I didn't want anyone coming in while I was in the shower." I'm cold from the frozen shower or maybe my anxiety just made my voice that detached. I grab the towel from Matteo.

"Why were you in the shower?" How do you explain anxiety about the unknown to your new boss. Plus, I don't want anyone getting in trouble for the comments they made when they thought I couldn't hear. "Why are you freezing?" Matteo asks at the same time as Mr. Segreto.

I don't answer. They seem to already know based on the looks they are throwing each other. Probably because of Tony. "Mario, can you please get a ginger ale and a plain bagel?" Mario looks at me, so I nod. Even though he answers to them, we've become close and he won't leave until I let him know it's safe.

"Since we have you, can we go over your integration into the business plan?" I nod. Hopefully, they won't ask any more questions. "First, we are going to split the companies Hal had between the three prior heads. They know you will be taking over a large chunk of them, but this way you can learn what you need to before being on your own."

"I thought I was going to help manage the crossover work and employees. Specifically with the financial aspects. I didn't think I was going to be a boss." Great, this talk is making me worse. I really need to leave or I'm going to do something unforgettable. Like drop my towel and start pacing in front of them with a broken office door. Maybe I should have gotten dressed before we started talking but clothes are not my friend right now.

"Why don't we have Mario take you back to the house and we can come up with a full written plan for you?" Mr. Segreto seems to know what's about to happen since he's guiding me back to the bathroom.

Matteo looks confused. "Dad. This is minor. I don't think we need a plan. Dani, you will be running the joint financial aspects, but you are fully legit. So, we can have you run the legitimate companies, which will keep your hands clean and take loads off myself and Tony. We also were thinking…". A hand to the back of his head stops his thought process. "What was that for?"

Alright I guess he didn't get the message. "Maybe you should leave the two of us. Now." He gives Matteo a pointed look at the door. "Let us know when Mario gets back so you can take her home."

Without another word, Matteo leaves. "When did the anxiety start?" he asks so softly. "Tony has it. It started after his mother left then got worse after he was shot the first time. It got better after he learned about the warehouses ironically. But it's always been something he managed on his own. I don't even think he knows he has it."

"When my parents were killed. It calmed down a little before Alex was killed. I was doing fine until this morning with the new job." I leave out everything else. That the warehouse helps me too. The school therapist said I had issues when there was no control and that lines up with everything.

He just nods. We sit in silence, but when his phone dings he's handing me my clothes and closing the bathroom door. When I walk out of the bathroom, I find Matteo waiting for me instead.

"Mario is downstairs and he is ready to take you back to the house. He has to make one brief stop, but it'll be quick."

***

Mario pulls over and jumps out after locking the doors to keep me in. Usually, I'm annoyed, but I don't have the energy to be annoyed. I tried to eat the bagel, but it wasn't possible. The ginger ale only made me feel worse.

The bang from guns snaps me out of my thoughts. I see Mario grab his shoulder. He is trying to fire back, but he can't lift his arm. I jump out of the car window. Locked doors are not going to keep me from helping. I grab the gun Mario is trying to fire and shoot the attacker. I get Mario into the passenger seat. Then I grab the attacker and throw him in the trunk. At least he's a small guy.

I grab a towel from the trunk to give Mario as I run to the driver's seat. My phone is on speaker. "Mr. Segreto? Should I take Mario to the hospital if he's been shot or somewhere else?"

"If he's conscious, the house. Are you hurt?"

"I'm fine. I need some help with directions." I hear him shouting away from the phone something about hacking the car. I didn't know you could do that, but sure. Seems reasonable. The navigation pops up and starts providing me with directions. "Thanks. I'll meet you there. Can you call doc?"

"You are not hanging up." I thought he would honestly.

I look at Mario who is paling. I push my hand against the wound and he moans. "I'm fine. Focus on the road." I get these men are used to getting their way, but why they think they can boss me around is funny. I push my hand harder against his shoulder since it seems to be helping. Not his pain, but the blood loss factor.

"Make sure doc brings blood. Also, you are now on speaker. Along with Mario, we have a guest in the trunk who will need some attention."

Mario looks over at me like I've grown another head or maybe a third arm. The quick trip is quiet. I don't think anyone knows what to do with the knowledge that there is someone else with us. I'm not going to be the one to share that information until I get some more answers. As much as I want to hit all the potholes for the trunk guy, I don't for Mario.

As I pull onto the street, the gate opens for me to fly through. You can't take Jersey out of the girl even if you move her. "Get him first." I point to Mario's door before anyone can do anything. Navigation said it was a twenty-minute trip, but I got here in under ten.

Three of the men who were waiting in the driveway gently carry Mario inside. Mr. Segreto is standing by the open door watching and directing everything. I guess this isn't the first time someone was brought here after being shot since they don't ask where to go and just move. I can't be of any help to Mario or the doc, so I guess I'll handle the one thing I can help with.

Three men rush past Mr. Segreto and look like they want to help get me inside. I open the trunk and the shooter is still out. I roll him out of the trunk and straight to the ground. I grab him by the arm and start dragging him towards the house.

"Stop! You are getting his blood everywhere!" I stop and look at the mess I've made. There is a small blood trail leading from the car trunk to me. That's going to be hard to get out. Not impossible though. "Go. Bring him to one of the warehouses. Don't kill him. We'll be there when we know Mario is alright."

I drop him arm as the men pick him up and put him back in the trunk. My eyes are on Mr. Segreto who looks pissed. "Cola gets blood out and it will just wash away." I start walking towards the house when his gaze shifts above me. I turn around and see a car flying inside the gate. I must have looked just like that. The windows are all tinted so I can't see the driver, but nobody is yelling or drawing guns.

The car isn't even stopped before the passenger is out of their door and running straight to me. Tony is spinning around me while assessing. I bet he is trying to find the cause of the blood since I'm covered in it. My hands have at least three layers with both Mario's and the shooter's. "Not a single scratch. It's not my blood." I say it softly so he knows it true but loud enough for his dad to also hear.

I grab his hand and pull him up the stairs. I need to see Mario. If something happens to him, it's on me even if nobody else thinks that. I just hope I made the right decision coming here instead of going to the hospital. When we reach his father, he turns and leads us further into the house. I think he knows what I need since nothing is said.

"Just a few more minutes boss and you will have my complete attention." Basically, don't fucking talk, I'm concentrating. I don't know how I feel about doc. Part of me likes that he is willing to do house calls, but I don't know how he got into this situation.

I ignore doc and go check on Mario. He's asleep which is good and his color is getting better. It's going to be a long night with not much sleep. I look around the room and there are at least five men I've never seen before in here.

I leave the room and go to the kitchen. Luckily Maria is still here. "Hi hun, can I get you something?"

"I'm fine right now." It's like she doesn't notice all the blood on me. "I have a felling we are going to have a larger group around for the next few days. Are you able to make extra servings?" Knowing the men, none of them will think about finding food until we're all hangry.

"Already on it. I have a few different options for tonight. Tomorrow morning, I'll see how many we are expecting and get a plan." She smiles over her shoulder at me. "Thanks for asking. They just assume I know how many for dinner." I mean, she is magical, but she does have enough sense for caring and feeding all these guys.

I walk back into the room. Everyone moved into the living room when I was in the kitchen. I grab a chair and sit next to Mario. He's still asleep but looks much better than he did. Hopefully, it's a quick healing process and he won't have any permanent damage.

Soft fingers brush my hair off my check. I don't remember falling asleep, but I watched the sun set through the window while monitoring his breathing. "Mostriciattola, wake up. Let's get you cleaned up and fed. Then you can come back and sit with Mario." I don't want to leave him alone, but another guy came in with Tony and is now in my seat.

Chapter 24

Tony

I get Dani out of her clothes and into the warm shower. She just stands under the spray of water and I see the tears start to fall. I climb in after her and start with her hair. She keeps crying even as I wash her body. When I rinse her off, I turn the water off and wrap her in a towel. Carrying her to the bed, I keep her in my lap and let her finish.

"What do you want to eat?" I ask softly pushing her hair off her face.

She just shakes her head. I pull out my phone and text one of my guys to bring food up. I don't care if someone sees her like this since it proves to my men that she will protect and care for them.

"What do you need?" She's going to need to sleep soon. I can tell she is on fumes.

"It should have been me." She sniffs. I was hoping I'd have a little time before her guilt started.

"Did you pull the trigger? Did you tell him to stand where he was standing?" She shakes her head after every question. "How is it your fault?"

"He was protecting me. He was there because of me." She's too used to be a lone wolf.

"He was doing his job. He was there because he was making a stop, not because of you. He protected you which is his job. If you got shot, he would feel terrible and it might have been his life. You were able to not only get him here safe, but you disarmed and captured his shooter. I can't tell you how pissed I am that you did something so risky, but I understand. Mario is going to be fine."

I hear the knock on our door, but I wait until she acknowledges what I said. "Enter." I see the tray full of options. "Thank you."

"Can you try to eat something and then I'll have doc give you a full update on Mario?" Bribery will get you everywhere.

She tries a little bit of everything before pushing the tray away. I walk her back to Mario's room, but stop at the doorway.

"Doc." He quickly leaves and joins us. "Can you please give Daniella an update?"

"Sure. He's doing great. It was a through and through. Blood loss, but that was handled. He's going to need to be on light duty for about a week and should take it easy overall."

She nods and he walks away. Hopefully, this will help her ease the guilt. Then I can get her to eat more and sleep. I put her back in the chair I found her in with a kiss on her head before walking out.

I need to talk to Matteo to see what happened to the shooter.

***

Sneaking out of bed is harder than I thought it'd be. Since Dani is usually up first, I never have to sneak out. Or if we wake each other up, neither of us is sneaking out.

I couldn't sleep last night anyway. I was too worried about screwing up today. Everything that can go wrong, I'm ready for it. I've gone through every situation that could happen and know how to handle it. After Dani fell asleep, I went down to the gym to work out my anxiety and when I came back, she was awake and waiting for me. I couldn't tell her why my mind is so loud.

I've been up for an hour. Breakfast is cooked and in the oven to stay warm. A fresh pot of coffee is on. Not that I need any more caffeine. Her mother's ring is burning in my pocket. I'm worried I'll lose it even though I keep checking for it every five seconds. I set up the table on the patio for us and started the fire so it would be comfortable.

"Why are you cooking? Where's Maria?" Shit. I didn't tell my dad what I have planned. He's not going to be happy that I told Maria to take the day off so I could cook breakfast and dinner.

"I gave her the day off. She's been working a lot with everything that has been going on and I figured I can handle cooking today." I shrug to keep him from asking more questions.

"That's true. You hate cooking though. What do you have planned?" I turn back and pull the potatoes out of the oven. "You wouldn't propose without talking with me first."

The words sound like a question, but the tone begs to differ. "I'm proposing this morning, which is why I'm cooking breakfast and then the four of us are having dinner to celebrate with the family sauce." Geez. I would crack so quickly under pressure if it was my dad asking questions. He wouldn't have to ask anything before everything spilled out.

He raised Matteo and I so we would never lie to him, but we are adults now and do keep some things to ourselves. I knew I should have told him about the proposing, but I was worried he'd say it's all too quick.

"She's a great fit for you. Let me know what her answer is. But I'm going to need my own plate before she comes down and eats all of this." I load a plate for him and add some cheese to his eggs. "I'm going into the office as soon as I'm finished. What time are you planning dinner for?"

"Five thirty." I make up two more plates since I hear footsteps.

She comes flying though the doorway, but freezes when she sees my dad eating. "Good morning."

"Morning. I'll see you two later. I have a lot I need to get done. Since Mario is still recovering, don't leave the house for the day." Dani just gives him a look, but dad's eyes are locked on mine.

165

"See you for dinner." Dani eyes are now on me, but my dad gives me a smile so she doesn't see it. I'm happy he's on board with this. After we talked, I figured he wanted her to be with me, but he also knows she could take me down if I hurt her.

"What's all of this for?" She asks as I get her into her chair at the patio table.

"I wanted to do something nice. I know we haven't been able to do many normal things like go on dates. So, I made us breakfast." I made sure I had everything situated before she got down.

"Uh-huh. And why are you dressed?" Great, she knows something is up.

I pull at my chair, but I don't sit. I grab the plates and put one at my seat before walking over to her. I put her plate in front of her before kneeling down on one knee. "Because I want you to marry me. I want to wake up next to you. Fall asleep with you. I can't imagine you not being in my life. Will you be wife? The mother of our children?"

I see tears, but I can't read anything else. She starts to shake her head. I deflate. Why not? "No?" I choke out.

"No. Yes, I'll marry you." She looks at me with the biggest smile possible.

"Yes?"

"Yes." She nods and dives into my arms. She kisses me before I pull back to wipe her tears away. I take the ring out of the box and place it on her finger. "How did you get my mom's ring?" The tears start again.

"Your brother left it with Matteo for whomever wanted to marry you." She kisses me again. This time more urgently. We don't get a single bite of our breakfast, but I carry her back to the room. I'd love to take her on the patio, but this is my father's house and she wouldn't allow it.

Once we get into our bedroom, I take her fast. As soon as the door closes, I rip off her clothes and mine. Without a second thought, I let her push me onto the bed. As she climbs over me, I follow her leave and lay down. This is her day.

I watch her take my entire length in at once and grind down. She starts slow, but quickly speeds up. As soon as her orgasm starts, I roll her under me. In less than three thrusts, I'm following her over the edge.

As soon as we both finish, I collapse next to her. The silence is nice. The leisurely touching is soothing. Soft kisses. Explorative touches. We've seen each other naked more times I can count, but this feels different. This feels like our first time together.

"I know we started this talk, but where do you want to live? Now that we are getting married, I think we should start looking." I saw with her curled on my chest.

I want to keep her there, but she pushes up to look at me. "Probably close to your family. I do like Maria's cooking."

"We could just move in here." I offer even though I know she doesn't want to.

"No. I'll want to just drop the kids off so we can have date nights without them. I'm sure your father will enjoy having time with them by himself. Plus, I'd trust him with them. I also know Maria will make sure they have an actual meal instead of just whatever they want."

She never said she wanted kids, but the look in her eyes say she's ready for them. "You want kids?" I whisper.

"With you? Yes." She leans in to kiss me, but I devour her.

I roll her onto her back and position myself at her entrance. "Want to start now?"

"Wedding first. Also, not when your father is home." I trust into her as she finishes that sentence.

I set a slow pace to drive her insane. This isn't the last time today, but we are going to need to get up at some point for the dinner I have scheduled with dad and Matteo.

I feel her start to climax and stop moving. I brush my lips against hers and pick up speed. I take her cries in my mouth so she's not worried someone else will hear. After she is full of me, I reach over and set an alarm before falling asleep with her wrapped in my arms.

***

When my alarm goes off, Dani groans. "Come on. We need to get up. I have a dinner to make." I pick her up and carry her to the bathroom.

"You can cook dinner?" Her hair is all over the place, which makes her look that much more fuckable. Showering together probably isn't the best idea, but I need to start the sauce.

We take a record-breaking shower and get dressed. Well, I got dressed. She got dressed, saw my outfit, and went back to change. I make sure the ring is on her finger and walk her to the kitchen. Since she is now a member of this family, she needs to learn the sauce.

"We are cooking dinner. You are in charge of pasta and I'm teaching you the family sauce." She looks at me like I've grown another head.

"Pasta takes like twenty minutes depending on the water. When are you planning to eat?"

I blink. "We don't use box pasta. You are making it from scratch. That's going to be easier than the sauce, but you still need to get started now. I have a feeling this is going to be an all-day event."

I pull out all the ingredients for her and get her situated before I pull out the sauce pot. Yes, we have a special pot for the sauce. I'm just realizing the amount of dairy though. Dani isn't going to be able to try it at all. I would just substitute stuff but it's not just cheese. It has heavy cream as its base. I can still teach her even if she can't eat it. We'll make new recipes when we have kids.

I didn't realize making pasta was going to be this messy. Growing up, Matty and I made pasta every week and it never turned into this. There is flour everywhere. I'm not even sure what type of pasta we will be eating. I stole a piece to test it and it came out perfect. I just need to clean this up before Maria gets here.

"You keep working on that sauce. I'm going to clean up whatever happened."

168

"I'll take care of it, mostriciattola." I try to push her towards the stools, but she stops.

She turns and looks up at me. "I made this mess on your behalf, but I need to do something and it definitely isn't making the sauce. I will clean up and get changed. Again. When your dad and brother arrive, it can't look like we had a flour fight."

I can't argue with that. She somehow makes the kitchen look cleaner than it did when I woke up this morning. Not that Maria will find that out.

I don't know why I wanted to do a celebratory dinner. Dad found out this morning. Matteo knew since I needed the engagement ring. But having them here, it's our first official family dinner together. Dad is shooting daggers at Dani. She hasn't touched the sauce that dad, Matteo, and I demolished as soon as we were all served.

"What's wrong with the family sauce?" Matteo and I drop our forks and sit up straight. Dad broke out his no-nonsense voice.

Dani levels him with a look. Completely unfazed by his temper. "I'm sure nothing is wrong with it. However, with all the dairy, I don't want to spend the night I got engaged puking." He nods, accepting that answer, which is the complete truth. She watched as I put more and more cream and cheese into the sauce.

"I guess it's time I present your engagement gift." My dad pulls out a small box. I have no idea where he hid that during dinner. Instead of handing it to me, he gives it to Dani. When he arrived home, he pulled her in for a bear hug. My father isn't a hugger, but with Dani, it seems all norms are gone.

"You didn't have to get us anything." Dani says even if her eyes look thrilled. As she opens it, I look at Matteo. He's thrilled, but I still see the sadness in his eyes. This was supposed to be him and Alex. He's been different lately. Ever since Dani brought her brother's things here to help Matteo, he's been content, almost happy.

I look in the box in Dani's hands. It has an old fashion key. We both look at my dad because this is weird. "It's for your house. I bought each of you a home for when you were ready to settle down. All you have to do is furnish it. I have a security team coming over next week to go over options with you two."

I guess our house hunting was a waste. "Thanks dad." "No. This is too much." I say at the same time Dani opens her mouth. That wasn't the right thing to say.

"Daniella, it isn't too much. This way I know you are both safe and I know you are close enough so I can see my grandkids whenever I want to." She starts to shake her head. "It's not an option. You will accept the house. Make it yours. Whatever you want."

Now, the tears are flowing. I thought we were done with the tears. "Mostriciattola, please. Your tears are killing me." That doesn't help.

My dad walks around the table and slides Dani's chair so it faces him instead of the table. "You are a part of this family. We protect each other. To do that, I need to know you are close by and safe. I know you can buy your own house, but this is something off your plate." He kisses the top of her head and she dives into his arms.

Epilogue – six months later

Daniella

I'm nervous. This is the first big family gathering we are hosting. I had to learn Italian cooking and not screwing up the family sauce recipe. Not that it is written down anywhere because that's too risky.

I made the pasta from scratch this morning with no problem, but I've been tinkering with the sauce all day. I keep bringing samples to Tony to see if I'm close. I can't tell if it's getting worse or not. After the first taste test, he's hidden his facial expressions from me.

I could use a glass of wine, but that's not possible even if I did drink. The reason for this dinner is the announcement. I told Tony at the three-month mark, we could share the news, but not sooner. With everything going on, the stress was too much and I wanted to make sure we were safe before telling them about the baby.

It's like he heard my thoughts and left his office. Hugging me from behind, he rests his hands on my stomach. I'm not showing, but we both can tell someone is growing in there. "I'm so excited to tell them. Do we have to wait until dessert?" He sounds like a toddler himself.

I might have told him we will sit on the news. I know it's mean, but morning sickness sucked and I need some level of joy. Torturing him is my

171

favorite thing. "If they don't figure it out before dessert then yes, you have to wait. The meal should tell them."

I haven't told him that his father knows. He hasn't said anything to me, but he might have caught me getting sick in the middle of the day because morning sickness isn't only in the morning. Moving meetings around without questioning it. But the best part is his observation of my cravings. He made sure to stock everything I'd been eating in the employee café area. Then, he had my wet bar converted into my own café when the snacks were going quickly in the general area.

After getting married, Mr. Segreto kept me on to run the legal businesses. I help with the administrative goings of all the businesses, but I only touch the legit ones. Tony tried to move my office closer to his, but when I resisted, his dad agreed with me. Tony and Matteo are pissed that I'm the favorite child. Even if they agree.

We got married in the backyard of our house since the priest wouldn't marry us in the church since I wasn't fully Catholic. Whatever that means. We had a quick ceremony, ate lunch together, then promptly kicked everyone out so we could enjoy each other. The wedding had to wait because the house took longer for the security features Tony insisted on, which I agree with. No need to not be over-secure.

The smells snap me back to reality. Something isn't right. I rush to the stove only to find Tony pouring different things into the sauce. "What are you doing?" I love the man, but he does not know what to do in the kitchen, except eat.

"Mostriciattola, you are amazing at so many things, but cooking the family sauce is not one of them."

I shouldn't be offended, but. "There is no recipe. I've never even had it! How the hell should I know what's in it?" I yell at him. Another thing with pregnancy, emotions are crazy. All the hormones. Tony doesn't seem to mind, just rolls with the punches. Sometimes literally.

That's when the smell catches up to my stomach. Oh no. I thought I was past this. I run to the bathroom. After the first time, Tony doesn't follow me anymore. I might have bitten his head off. He was trying to be helpful and supportive, but it pushed into overprotective mode for me. Once we calmed down and I explained it, he agreed to not follow me unless I asked him to.

The alarm rings letting us know approved guests passed the gate. I go to the front door to welcome them since they don't knock all the time. You'd think after catching us having sex a few times, they would alert us that they were coming or knock, but no. So, I had the security team come back and set up alarms when someone crossed onto our property.

I open the front door and watch Mr. Segreto bring in a small gift bag, clearly aware of what this dinner is for. He gives me the biggest, longest, and gentlest hug ever before kissing my cheek. "I can't wait to meet the little one. When's he due?"

Tony is convinced it's a boy as well. Me, I'll wait for the test results. "We don't know it's a he. Today is the three-month mark." He pulls me in for another hug, but the alarm sounds again. "Why didn't Matteo drive with you?" We try to drive together as often as possible, safety in numbers or something like that.

"It's a boy." He says with his boss voice. "He said he had to pick something up first." He shrugs and stands next to me.

We watch as Matteo parks behind Mr. Segreto and gets out of the car. I don't know why he stopped at the passenger door, though. "Tony, come here." I yell into the house. Away from Mr. Segreto's ear. The first time they heard me yell, they all couldn't hear for a week, so now I'm careful.

"Hey dad. What's with the gift?" Before his father can I answer, we freeze. Matteo brought a date to our family dinner, which is strange. Tony and his dad look pissed, but I can't contain my happiness. This is exactly what Alex would want for him.

"Go set another place seating. Your father already figured out the news, so you two shoo." I send them away so I can have a few minutes with Matteo first.

ACKNOWLEDGMENTS

Jess: Thanks for being the best no questions asked supporter

Kiersten: Thank you for encouraging this dream

Readers: Thank you for letting me share this with all of you

ABOUT THE AUTHOR

AP Greene is:
A dog mom, aunt, sister, daughter, friend, both a book dragon and worm.

She uses writing as a form of therapy and guarantees a happily ever after in
every book. She loves to focus on emotional relationships with her main
characters.

www.ingramcontent.com/pod-product-compliance
Lightning Source LLC
Chambersburg PA
CBHW071717140626
46557CB00012B/942